TH

It's lust at first
ters Lance, a sexy ...
New York's premier private kink club.

She's happy for the distraction, since she recently left her lover. Unfortunately, her session with Lance is cut short when her boss, Kingsley Edge, reveals they're all in danger....

THE ORIGINAL SINNERS PULP LIBRARY

Vintage paperback-inspired editions of standalone novels and novellas from *USA Today* bestseller Tiffany Reisz's million-copy selling Original Sinners erotic romance series. Learn more at tiffanyreisz.com.

THE ORIGINAL SINNERS
PULP LIBRARY

THE
LAST
GOOD
KNIGHT

THE LAST GOOD KNIGHT

TIFFANY REISZ

8TH CIRCLE PRESS • LOUISVILLE, KY

Previously published by Harlequin Books/Mills & Boon as the serialized novella *The Last Good Knight: I—V*

Cover design by Andrew Shaffer

Front cover image contains a photo used under license from iStock by Getty Images

Mass-Market Paperback ISBN: 978-1-949769-21-0

Also available as an ebook from 8th Circle Press and as an audiobook series from Harlequin Audio

First Edition

For those readers keeping track, this erotic suspense story takes place three years before the first full-length Original Sinners novel, The Siren. *It does, however, stand on its own.*

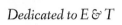

Dedicated to E & T

CONTENTS

"I can do it. Try it again." Nora took a deep breath, followed by a deeper drink of her vodka and tonic.

"Mistress, this is the fourth time." Simone gave her a pleading look. "Are you sure?"

"I'm sure. I got it this time. I'm ready. Do it, sub. Go."

"Okay, okay." Simone ran a hand through her rainbow-colored hair and looked Nora in the eyes. "How old are you?"

Nora stared at Simone without blinking. "I am..."

"You can do it, Mistress."

The ice in Nora's glass rattled in her hand. "Thirty."

"Holy shit!" Simone applauded. She threw her arms around Nora and gave her a kiss on the cheek. "Good job!"

"Oh, my God, that was hard." Nora rubbed

her temples. "I hate being thirty. I swear I was in my twenties a week ago."

"You *were* in your twenties a week ago."

"That explains it. Thank you. I needed a little help getting to stage five in the grieving process."

"Stage five?"

"Acceptance."

"Happy to help you find acceptance anytime, Mistress." Simone leaned against Nora's shoulder, and Nora kissed her on top of her multicolored hair. With or without rainbow-striped hair, Simone would have been attractive, but no one could miss that mass of soft, flowing hair cascading down her back in an array of bright colors.

"What the hell do you use on your hair, anyway? Kool-Aid?"

Simone giggled, and Nora decided she had probably earned a beating tonight. Simone looked up at her with eager eyes and the Mistress pressed a long kiss onto her carmine-colored lips. Maybe the rainbow-hued sub had earned more than a beating.

"If you ask nicely, I might beat you *and* fuck you," Nora said against Simone's lips.

Simone groaned, but not in an erotic way. "I can't, Mistress. I'm booked." She looked heartbroken, devastated, and miserable. And utterly adorable.

"Who booked you? I'll kill him."

Simone shrugged and shook her head. "I don't

know. Mr. King told me I was needed in the bar at ten, which is—"

"Now," came a familiar voice from behind Nora. She didn't turn around. She didn't need to. She'd know that cold, pretentious, overeducated voice anywhere. "Simone, shall we?"

"Yes, Mr. S.," Simone said, and Nora could tell she was trying not to smile—not in front of the Mistress anyway. The only person Simone enjoyed subbing for more than Nora was Søren, and Søren was her ten o'clock. Well, wasn't that just peachy?

"Eleanor..." Søren said and Nora refused to turn around and look at him.

"Søren. Have a lovely evening."

"I certainly plan to. Excuse us."

Simone shot Nora a final apologetic glance as she took Søren's proffered arm like a lady with her squire. No one could play the part of the gentleman better than Søren, but it was all an act. She and Simone knew that from personal experience. When he shut the dungeon door behind him, the gentleman turned into a sadist and all pretense of chivalry died. Thank God. Søren was no gentleman and she was no lady. And that's how it should be down here.

Out of the corner of her eye, she watched Simone disappear from The 8th Circle's VIP bar. She kept her eyes lowered respectfully, her posture submissive, but Nora saw the pleasure of anticipation gleaming in her eyes. By day, Simone worked on her Ph.D. in International Relations. She paid for that expensive education with money earned on the floor and in the dungeons of Kingsley's S&M clubs. But Simone never charged Søren a penny for his hour with her. With Søren it was always pleasure, never business. Nora knew that Simone and almost every other submissive at the Circle would pay *him* for the privilege of a beating. And to think once upon a time, Nora belonged to him—heart, body, and soul. And she'd given it up for this. For freedom.

And it was worth it. At least that's what Nora told herself.

Nora spun on the barstool and gazed around the club. A quiet night, as weeknights usually were. Quiet*er,* anyway. Only two hundred or so deviants floating about instead of the usual five hundred on Friday and Saturday nights. But this was a school night. Half the members of the club were married and had kids. At least ninety percent of her clientele were married men who'd rather lie to their wives and come to Nora to explore their fetishes than tell the truth to the women they'd pledged to love and honor. It was a good thing, too. If the wives of the world were a little more open-minded about male submission and fetishes, where would she be?

Out of a job.

Feeling frustrated by Simone's abrupt departure, Nora took another drink of her vodka. Maybe she should call it a night, go home, get some sleep.

She might even get up early tomorrow and work on her new book. Kingsley didn't let her have much in the way of free time these days, now that her career as a dominatrix had taken off. In two years she'd become the go-to gal for all things kink. The money poured in. The pain poured out. Days off were few and far between.

As she hopped off her stool, the elevator at the end of the bar rose. Maybe Kingsley had decided to come up for air finally. She hoped so. She wanted to chew him out for sending Simone to Søren when Nora had already decided that Simone would belong to her tonight. Not that Kingsley had known that, but Nora never missed an opportunity to drive Kingsley halfway up the wall. Maybe she'd make him take Simone's place on her St. Andrew's Cross tonight.

But no, it wasn't Kingsley who stepped out of the elevator. It was a different man—one she'd never seen before. He wore black jeans and black boots, a red T-shirt stretched over his broad chest. He had a good tan, short dark hair, and a handsome face—handsome in a rugged sort of way with half a day's stubble and troubled eyes. Troubled? Interesting. *Nervous* she might have expected, especially since he seemed to be new. But troubled? That was a mystery she had to solve.

The man came up to the bar and ordered a boring American beer. With nonexistent effort he popped the top off and drank it in a few easy swallows. She noticed a handkerchief tucked in his back pocket—black on white: a submissive looking for a dominant. This evening was starting to look up.

"Military," she said, walking over to the barstool next to him. "Am I right?"

"Is it the haircut?" he asked.

"And the really good posture. Let me guess... Army Ranger. All you guys are kinky fuckers."

He laughed a little.

"I'm insulted."

"Oh, insulted, are you? Gotta be a Marine, then."

He shook his head. "Keep guessing."

"That's 'Keep guessing, *Mistress*' to you."

He swiveled on his stool and for the first time looked straight at her. She wore black thigh-high boots decorated with a dozen silver buckles, a red leather skirt, red corset, black jacket, and a black top hat complete with a red band. She looked amazing and she knew it. Kingsley had gotten the best tailor in the city to design her fetish wardrobe. Yet another reason she'd been looking for a little play tonight. Shame to waste such a good outfit on an evening of celibacy.

"Keep guessing, Mistress." He bowed his head in deference.

"Only one type of military more proud of themselves than the marines. Navy SEAL?"

He said nothing. Only sipped at his beer.

"I knew it. SEAL," she said. "Give me a second to pat myself on the back."

She reached her arm around her shoulder and swatted herself awkwardly.

"This is harder than it looks," she said. "Don't laugh at me." Nora switched arms and tried patting herself from around and behind her back. "I'm going to keep doing this until you admit you're a SEAL."

She crossed her arms over her face and then stretched back to pat herself again. Her breasts nearly popped out of her corset.

He laughed even harder. "Fine. Just stop that before you hurt yourself," he said, a broad grin taking over his face and a twinkle shining in his dark blue eyes.

Nora immediately dropped her arms to her sides. "Whew. Thank you. That was getting weird fast."

"For both of us."

"What are you doing at my club, Mr. Navy SEAL? I know it's not Fleet Week. I have Fleet Week marked on my calendar. And my underwear."

"It's Mr. Ex-Navy SEAL. And I'm here because I was told to come tour the place, enjoy myself and see if I liked it."

"You do like it, don't you?" Nora rested her chin on her hand and waggled her eyebrows at him.

"It's definitely...entertaining?" He turned the word into a question. She didn't blame him. Hard to find the right word to describe The 8th Circle.

Most days she just called it home. "Nice floor show."

"I'll be here all week." Nora held out her hand. "I'm Mistress Nora. Nice to beat you."

Instead of shaking her hand, he took it delicately and brought it to his lips for a kiss.

"An honor to serve you, Mistress Nora. I'm Lance."

"Would you like to serve me, Lance? I haven't been served all week." She gave him a wide smile, a smile with a promise, a promise she fully intended to keep.

"Someone should serve a woman like you every single day, or as often as you desire, of course."

She took her top hat off and set it on the bar. Without pretense or shame, she perused his body. One good thing about being a dominatrix—she got to have as much fun as the men of this world did. Dominatrixes weren't just *allowed* to treat men like sexual objects, they were expected to. Hell, they were even paid to. Down here the dominatrixes were treated like queens. Even the male dominants usually gave them wide berth. Every male dominant except for a certain arrogant six foot four blond she'd like to see on her cross one of these days. Kink or crucifixion, either one worked for her.

"You're good at this," she said, impressed by his attitude.

Lance leaned in a few inches and lowered his voice. "I've had a little practice, Mistress."

The Mistress raised her chin. "Only a little? You need a lot more practice than that. Wanna go practice?"

"We just met."

"Are you calling me a slut because I asked you to play?" She batted her eyelashes at him.

"No, ma'am. Never." His laugh reached all the way to his dark blue eyes. She loved a man who could laugh.

"Am I calling *you* a slut by asking you to play?"

"You can call me anything you want."

The Mistress placed a hand on Lance's thigh and felt the hard muscle under the denim.

"You looked troubled when you came in here. And your entire body is tense. I'd like to flatter myself that you're hard all over because of me, but you looked uncomfortable before you saw me. What's up?"

Lance nodded at the bartender who brought him another beer. "I haven't played in a long time. I'm not even sure if I should be here."

"Should you be here? Or did you sneak in?"

"I just got a job working for Kingsley Edge."

"Never heard of him." Nora kept a straight face. Kingsley tried to keep employees from fraternizing with each other too much, a hopeless cause where Nora was concerned. Lance must be the new house manager he'd hired. It would take someone with a military background to keep Kingsley's coterie under control.

"He's some rich kinky bigwig. Owns this place. Club membership is one of the fringe benefits."

"You like it here?"

"I feel a little out of place. My first time in a club like this."

"A club full of rich and famous perverts?"

"Exactly. I'm neither. Well, not the rich and famous part, anyway. Pervert maybe. This is definitely not my usual crowd."

A congressman on the leash of a domme crawled on all fours past the bar.

"Don't worry. They're not my crowd, either. Don't be intimidated." She leaned forward and crossed her legs. "I'll let you in on a secret. The top dominant here is a Jesuit priest, and he comes here in his clerical collar all the time. Jesuits take a vow of poverty. Everyone defers to him even though he's not rich. He earned that respect. No one has ever ratted him out."

"That's a comfort, Mistress. Nice to feel safe."

"You are safe down here. And you're with me. I'll protect you from the rich and famous perverts."

"My hero," he said, turning toward her so that their lips were only an inch apart.

"Come on, Lance," she whispered. "Come play with me. Submit to me. You know you want to. I know you want to. You're not on duty right now, are you?"

"No." He shook his head. She could see him trying to bite back a smile.

She moved her hand from his thigh to his crotch and felt his erection.

Lance closed his eyes and inhaled sharply.

"What do you want to do, sailor?"

"Anything you want, Mistress. Anything at all."

"That's a dangerous word around here. Let's go find out what you mean by *anything*."

She slipped off the barstool and patted her thigh. Lance threw a tip down on the bar and followed. The 8th Circle had a two-drink maximum, and booze and tips were included in the price of admittance. He didn't have to pay a thing, didn't have to leave a tip. But he did it anyway. Most of the rich sons of bitches who played here were misers. Real men like Lance knew the value of a hard day's work and left good tips. She liked that. That ten-dollar tip on a seven-dollar tab had just earned him the chance to fuck her. Tonight she'd let him fuck her first then tell him why after. Hmm...she kind of liked that line. She'd put it in a book someday.

He followed her in silence out of the bar and down the stairs to her dungeon in the Hall of the Masters, as it was known. Kingsley had envisioned The 8th Circle as the BDSM club to end all BDSM clubs. He'd have the world's most beautiful dominatrixes and submissives—male and female—on his staff with permanent dungeons. Plus the members could earn the right to their own private quarters. Of course, Kingsley and Søren got the two best suites in the place. Not that she could complain about her dungeon. Kingsley had turned what was once a pit into a palace. She was the queen around here, after all. Nothing less than the best for her.

They passed an open door to one of the dungeons. Inside a young woman lay curled on the floor, her eyes rimmed with tears as she pleaded for mercy. A man twice her size grabbed her by her hair.

Lance took a step toward the door and Nora stopped him with a hand on his chest.

"Whoa there, sailor. Don't interrupt."

"But she's—"

"Having the time of her life. That's Alexis. She loves getting treated like a slave. The rougher you are with her, the more she cries, the happier she is."

"Sorry..." Lance wrenched his gaze from the open door. "I'm sorry, Mistress. It's hard for me to see women crying or in pain."

"You've never been in a BDSM club with female submissives before?"

"Never. I know it happens. Just never seen with my own eyes."

"It's all good fun. Don't worry. Her husband is one of the most thoughtful, careful dominants I know. He takes good care of her. And I promise my dungeon is currently free of crying women. Usually, it's the men crying around me."

"They're married? Seriously?" Lance asked, nodding toward the door.

"Happily. Can't you tell?" Nora asked as they reached her dungeon. At her door, Nora pulled the scarf out of Lance's back pocket and tied it around the doorknob. She didn't know Lance so she had no plans to lock the door. The scarf would signal that the Mistress was in session and all would do well to leave them the hell alone. Plus, when Søren had finished with Simone, he'd come out, see the scarf on the knob, and know exactly what was happening inside. And there was jack-fucking-nothing he could do about it.

As she tied the scarf on the knob, Lance removed his shoes and socks.

"Undressing already?" she asked, not displeased.

"Just the shoes and socks. This is your private dungeon, yes?"

"Yes."

"Then it deserves to be shown respect."

"Lance, I like the way you kink." She opened the door and stepped inside. She loathed artificial light so she lit her oil lamp. Lance set his shoes right inside the doorway. Every little thing he did was endearing. The man had manners.

"So," Nora said as she ushered Lance into the room, "welcome to Hell. Like it?"

He gazed around the room with unabashed

appreciation. She did have nice digs, very French bordello style. Kingsley told her to decorate however she wanted. He probably regretted that once he saw the place. Bed—four-poster bed, of course —with a gold-and-red brocade bedspread, erotic artwork on the walls, a few oil lamps and candles, and condoms and handcuffs in every drawer.

"If this is Hell, I can't wait to see Heaven."

"Heaven's in this room." She snapped her fingers and waved her hand. Lance raised an eyebrow before entering the second room of her suite.

He let out an impressed whistle.

"My playroom. Isn't it pretty? We have twenty different styles and lengths of rope." She put her hand on her hip, doing her best Vanna White strut around the room. "Floggers of every style. Single-tails. I'm very good at whipping if you like whipping. St. Andrew's Cross, of course. Medical bed. This little case here has the violet wand. And my cabinet...well, I'll leave it to your imagination."

The cabinet housed most of the sex toys, the vibrators and butt plugs and cock rings, that sort of thing. But inside one could also find her edge-play toys—razor blades and other cutting implements.

"This is amazing, Mistress. Not sure I can afford you."

Nora came up to him and wrapped her arms around his shoulders. "I'm not planning on charging you. You wanna know why?"

"I'm that handsome, Mistress?"

She gave him a broad grin. Handsome, funny and a little cocky—she liked that combination.

"I've seen worse, but no client is so handsome he gets a freebie," she said. "No, the reason I'm not charging you is because...I don't fuck my clients. And I fully intend to fuck you tonight."

"I fully intend to let you, if it pleases you, Mistress."

"I think it pleases me. Now let's talk. What would please *you?*"

She pulled away from him and took a seat on the big wooden bondage throne. It took nothing more than a nod to get Lance to kneel on the floor at her feet.

"Nothing pleases me more than pleasing a powerful woman," he confessed. "I'd love to make you come over and over again."

"Good boy. Anything else? Do you like pain?"

"Do you like giving it, Mistress?"

"Yes. Very much."

"Then I like receiving it. Very much. You do have some beautiful whips."

Nora stroked her bottom lip as she studied him. Time for the little dance she did with the male submissives. They were so desperate to please their Mistress that it took a full-blown inter-rogation to get them to admit to her what their own desires were. Some male submissives who hated pain would agree to take it if they thought the Mistress wanted to give it. But Lance had mentioned the whips and called them *beautiful*.

Masochistic streak in him. Good. She might have to keep him.

Keep him? Where had that thought come from? She'd never collared a sub before, never kept one as her personal property. It was too much like having a boyfriend or, God forbid, a husband. But...she got a very good feeling from Lance. The man must have been six feet tall in shoes, solidly built, and muscular. He looked like he could break her in half if he had a mind to, but she felt safe around him. Wouldn't be any sort of torture to have this guy in her dungeon as often as possible.

"You like whips. See anything else you like?" she asked.

"Nice cross. Very nice."

"The wrist cuffs on it are adjustable. I've had tiny little girls on there and men even taller than you. Anything else you like?"

"You have an amazing crop collection, looks like." He nodded toward a wall where at least twenty different riding crops hung.

"I do. Go get one for me. Any crop you like. I'll show you a trick."

He rose and went to the wall of riding crops. Nora watched him as he scanned the options. "Do you mind if I...?"

"Be my guest."

He pulled a crop down and held it in one hand flat on his palm. Then with both hands, he gripped either end and bent it. He hung it back on the wall and did the same thing to the next crop. Interesting. He was testing them for their give. The looser the crop, the less it hurt when struck with it. The tighter the crop, the less yield to it, the more it hurt. She had some crops that were a step up from a wet noodle and others that were barely a step down from a rattan cane, a toy that could split the skin and put a sub in the hospital if used incorrectly. Not that she would ever do that. Not unless someone paid in advance for it.

"That black one with the white braiding has a steel spine under the leather," she said. "Hurts like fuck. So does that solid red one. Both of them are vicious."

"I like vicious." He pulled down the solid red one and tried to bend it. It had almost no give to it.

He brought it back to the throne and sat again at Nora's feet. "My lady," he said, handing her the crop.

"Lady?" She took the crop in her right hand. "No ladies allowed in my dungeon."

"I would never argue with the Mistress," Lance said, watching her twirl the crop like a baton over the right arm of the throne. It had taken her three solid months of practice before she mastered the twirl. "But I do see a lady in this room, the most beautiful lady I've seen in a long time. She's strong, smart, and completely comfortable with who and what she is. She also understands the men who want to serve at her feet."

"I'm going to beat the shit out of you tonight

and fuck you. And then probably fuck you again, and you call me a lady?"

"Yes, Mistress. Nothing unladylike about any of that. Not in my eyes."

Nora caught her crop and let it slide down between her fingers until she caught it by the handle.

She leaned forward and put the end of the crop handle under Lance's chin, forcing his mouth to meet her mouth. Their lips hovered only an inch apart.

"You know what, Lance? I think I like your eyes."

Just to be sadistic, Nora stayed there for a few unnecessary seconds, letting Lance feel her breath against his lips before she moved forward, closed the gap between them, and kissed him. The kiss started soft and careful but quickly turned passionate. She slipped her tongue into his mouth and bit his top lip. Even as the kiss deepened, grew hungrier, Lance stayed on his knees and kept his hands to himself. He wouldn't touch her without permission. Someone had trained this man and trained him well.

With reluctance, she pulled back from Lance. She'd almost forgotten how much she loved kissing a man. She had sex mostly with women lately, a nice break from the male clients she dealt with all day long. When was the last time she'd even kissed a man on the mouth? A month ago? Two? It would have been Kingsley, right? The last man she'd kissed? And he hadn't had a session with her in weeks. Kissing Lance, she realized how much she missed the feel of soft stubble on her skin, missed the sense of power restrained. If she didn't stop kissing him now, they'd end up making out all night instead of doing what she really wanted to do.

"Take your shirt off," she ordered. Lance hesitated. "Shy?" she asked.

"Not really. But I have some scars. Fair warning."

"I don't mind scars. Show me, sailor. That's an order."

He sat back on his heels and with one easy tug pulled his shirt up and off. Any other man would have simply tossed it on the floor, but he took the three extra seconds to fold it neatly before setting it at her feet like an offering. If she hadn't known he was military before, that would have done it.

"I don't see many scars." She looked and saw only a few random healed cuts here and there.

"Wrong side," he said.

Nora raised her eyebrow. She gripped him by the back of his neck and pulled him forward. At the base of his spine, she saw a thick mass of scar tissue.

"Damn. Bullet wound?" she asked.

"IED. Got hit with shrapnel. Looks ugly but it didn't hit the spine."

"Does it cause you any issues I need to know about?"

Lance narrowed his eyes at her. "The scar doesn't bother you, Mistress?"

She shrugged. "One of my best clients is riddled with bullet wounds. I just need to know if it gives you any pain or other issues that would impede or change our play."

"Just a little nerve damage in that area."

"Understood. I won't play anywhere near the scars then. Easy enough."

"I'm glad you're okay with the scars. I haven't really been...it's been a while."

"You have a gorgeous body, Lance. I don't say that to everyone. Just people with gorgeous bodies. I am a little shocked by one thing, however. Where are your tats? I can't believe I have a seaman in here with no tattoos," she teased as she caressed his bare chest with her fingertips.

"I don't need ink to advertise my service, Mistress. I know what I am. The Navy knows what I am. You know what I am. No one else needs to know."

She raised her eyebrow at him.

"Something wrong, Mistress?"

"Absolutely nothing."

The caress turned into a scratch as she ran her fingernails over the sensitive skin of his upper chest. She dug in a little deeper and left four red trails in his flesh. As she scratched he closed his eyes and leaned his head back, offering more of himself to her touch.

"Stand up. Go to the cross. Face it."

His years of military service had turned the man into an order-obeying machine. He came right to his feet, swiftly but without unnecessary or graceless expediency. He walked to the cross and stood facing it.

"So obedient...I need more of you boys in my life. I only have a couple of military clients. One Air Force pilot. One Marine. Some kind of officer. Nice guy. Loves getting his balls flogged."

"Sounds like the definition of being in the Marines to me."

"I need a Coastie. I haven't done nearly enough boat kink."

"I have a friend in the Coast Guard. I'll get you his number."

"I'd rather have your number, Lance. Pick a number between one and one hundred. Take your time to decide. I need to pick a whip."

Nora left him standing in front of the cross as she perused her single-tail collection.

"You're not going to tell me what I'm picking, Mistress?"

"Nope."

"Fifty."

Nora smiled as she picked out one of her heavier single-tails. "Smart. Split the difference. I might be having you pick out how many minutes we play in my bed tonight or I might be forcing you to choose how many lashes you get with this nasty bitch." She let the whip flick the cross about six inches from Lance's shoulder. She missed on purpose, hoping to see if he'd jump. He didn't.

"Seemed the smart choice," he said. "But I'll change my answer if you want me to."

"No...fifty is perfect." She reached into a drawer and pulled out a stopwatch. "Fifty is how many minutes I'm going to make you wait until I let you inside me. Starting...now." She programmed fifty minutes into her stopwatch and hung it on the wall by the cross.

Nora stood behind him and pressed her corset-covered breasts into his back.

"Do you wish you'd picked a different number? Maybe one?" she asked him as she wrapped the whip around his chest and pushed him back against her.

"One part of my body wishes I'd picked one. The rest of my body can live with fifty, Mistress. I'm a man with a good appreciation for foreplay."

"Foreplay. A good way to think of it. Ready to play?"

"Yes, Mistress."

"Good." She curled up her whip again and sat it on a table while she pulled out wrist cuffs. "Got a safe word?"

"I do. *Semper Fi.*"

"*Semper Fi?* Isn't that the motto of the Marines?"

"It is. Why do you think I equate it with surrender?"

"You know, my father was a Marine," Nora

said, cuffing Lance's left wrist to the cross. She had to get on a step stool to reach high enough.

Lance winced. "I'm sorry, Mistress. I have nothing but respect for the Corps. I've served with them, and they're all brave and honorable men and women. It's all good-natured rival—"

"I'm just fucking with you. My dad was a lowlife, two-bit crook who never made a legal cent in his life."

"You're the devil, Mistress." Lance sounded impressed.

"I might have forgotten to mention that. Glad you noticed." She cuffed his right wrist and picked up her whip again. Pausing, she took a moment to study his back. The scar tissue ended about six inches above his back belt loop. That tissue was tough, but she didn't want to fuck with surgical scars. Dominatrixes hurt but they didn't harm. She pictured landing the lashes from shoulder blade to shoulder blade and down to the second-to-last rib of his rib cage. With his arms bound high up on the cross, she could see all the taut muscle of his back and arms and count his ribs. The man had a beautiful back. All it wanted for was a few dozen welts.

"We use the red-yellow-green-light system down here." She unfurled the whip and held it by the handle in her right hand with the tip in her left. "At any point, call out any of those colors as needed. You say green and I'll give you more. You say yellow and I'll pull back the pace. You say red and I drop the whip and we play with a new toy. Got it?"

"Yes, Mistress."

"Good. Also, if you want, you can say 'Ouch.' And that won't stop anything at all."

At that she let the whip fly. She struck the dead center of his back between the shoulder blades. He flinched then—everyone did—but he didn't say "yellow" or "red." He didn't even say "Ouch."

She let the whip fly again and dusted his broad back with red welts. Like a good pain-artist, she let the whip dance over his skin, not landing in the same place twice in a row. That way he would never know where the next blow would land. He wouldn't be able to brace himself. She counted in her head as she whipped him—ten, twenty, forty, sixty. By sixty she started hearing "Ouch." By seventy it'd turned into "Fuck." At seventy-five she hit a sensitive spot hard enough for a genuine cry of pure pain. But still, she heard no *red*, no *yellow*.

"Green?" she asked as she gave him a minute to breathe. "I won't think any less of you if you say yellow or red."

"Still green..." His breathing had turned ragged. "I just need a minute, if it pleases you, Mistress."

"It pleases me. Read me how many minutes we have left."

Lance craned his neck to look at the stopwatch

hanging next to the St. Andrew's Cross. "Thirty-seven."

"Goodie. I stopped at seventy-five. Let's make it an even hundred. Then we'll play a new game. And maybe get rid of some more clothing. Yours."

"Anything you desire, Mistress."

She desired to give him twenty-five more lashes. Again the whip danced over his skin. She focused on his sides now and his shoulders. By the time she hit twenty his back had turned bright red. One welt even oozed a small amount of blood.

"Stay there," she said as she put her whip in the pile of toys needing to be cleaned. "We have breakage."

Lance peered back over his shoulder. "Much blood?" he asked, seeming entirely untroubled at the idea she'd broken the skin.

"Not much." She snapped on a pair of latex gloves and cleaned the small wound with Betadine and ointment. "Okay, we have two Band-Aid options—Snoopy or Sesame Street?"

"Snoopy," he said.

"Perfect." She applied the Band-Aid, tossed her gloves, and dropped a quick kiss onto the center of his back. The beating had left his skin burning. She felt the heat against her lips.

"You're good, Mistress." Lance turned back to face the wall. "I've never been with a domme who plays as hard as you."

"I appreciate that. I trained under the best sadist in the world."

"Interesting. What do you consider a good sadist, Mistress?"

Nora tapped her chin as she thought about the question.

"Talent is part of it," she said. "Takes a lot of talent to hurt someone without injuring them. A baseball bat can inflict pain, but it also breaks bones. How do you inflict real and serious pain but without causing harm? The sadist I learned from is amazing at that. He knows all the pain pressure points on the human body so he can cause you acute agony without leaving a single mark."

"We learned a lot of those in training. Good for self-defense."

"Good for kink," she said. "But it's more than talent. True, the man can kill a fly with the tip of a whip. But he can also break someone down in a way that...I don't know." She stopped and shook her head. "I don't know anyone who can put someone back together by breaking them apart the way he can. You leave him with your body limping and your heart soaring."

"Is that what you're doing to me?"

"Are you limping yet?"

"No, Mistress. Soaring."

Nora smiled at his back, smiled so he couldn't see it. If he kept this up she would collar him before the night was over and that would be about the worst idea in the history of the Underground. She'd left a man who'd collared her and tied her down. The last thing she'd ever do was chain someone up in the very bonds she'd escaped.

"Time check?"

"Twenty-eight minutes, Mistress."

"Oh, good. I'm getting horny."

"That would make two of us."

"Really? Prove it," she said as she unlocked first his right then his left wrist from the cross.

She stood back and waited, her arms crossed over her chest.

Lance unbuttoned his jeans and pushed them down. As he stood in his boxer briefs, he smoothed and folded his pants. She took them from him as he stripped out of his underwear. Now Nora whistled. The man had the most magnificent thighs she'd ever seen. A hard ridge of muscle traveled straight from his knee to his hip. She'd bite that muscle tonight and see if she chipped a tooth.

"I could die on your quads," she said. "Or between them. Seriously, can you crush coconuts with those thighs?"

"I'd say thank you but that's the last part of my body I was hoping you would notice, Mistress." He said the words with a rueful smile.

"Oh, I noticed that, too. Hard to miss it." She stepped forward and wrapped her hand around his thick, hard inches.

Lance gave a labored breath as she stroked him. He probably wanted her to take a firm grip and stroke harder, so instead she merely grazed him with her fingertips, touching him as lightly as possible. His stomach muscles contracted.

"How good is your orgasm control?" She teased the tip with one finger and felt fluid on her skin, a drop or two. She massaged it back into the head.

"Decent. You order me not to come, and I won't come. I can't last much longer than a week or two, though, or it'll happen in my sleep."

"How old are you?" She stroked the underside of his cock with the back of her hand.

"Thirty-six, Mistress."

"You've played with a domme before?"

"My first real relationship was with a domme." Lance closed his eyes as she cupped his testicles.

"Really? How old were you when you were with her?"

Lance opened his eyes and smiled at her. "Eighteen to twenty-two. College."

"Not many college girls are tough enough to top men. Takes a few years to get to that point." Nora wrapped her whole hand around him and tugged.

"This college girl was a beautiful, tall, dark-haired professor in her late thirties with a wicked mind and a wickeder flogging arm."

"Fucking a professor?" she said, stroking him harder to show her approval.

"She fucked me, Mistress. I might have been inside her, but it was always at her whim and command."

"My kind of gal. Anyone since then?" She kept stroking him, testing his endurance, his ability to keep himself from coming.

"Here and there. Only professionals since then. No one in the past six years."

"Why not?"

He sighed heavily. "I got married. Bad idea."

"Worst idea I've ever heard. Divorced?"

"Yes."

"Good. She wasn't kinky?"

"Just so you know, Mistress, talking about my marriage is the best orgasm control there is. If we talk about it, I can guarantee I won't be coming anytime soon."

Laughing, she took the hint. She could tell there was a lot more to that story, but she didn't press him for it. He didn't come down to her dungeon for a therapy session. Pain and sex were on the menu tonight. They'd save the getting to know each other bullshit for later.

"Since I do want you coming at some point tonight, I'll ask you about your ex-wife another time when I'm feeling really sadistic. For now how about you follow me..." Without letting go of him, she took a step back and led him slowly and carefully to a leather-covered kneeling bench, not unlike the kind found at prayer shrines.

"I'll follow anywhere you lead, especially if you have my cock in your hand."

"Stay here. I'll get the stopwatch. We don't

want to go into overtime on the pain and miss all the fucking."

"No, Mistress, we absolutely do not."

She heard a bit of a drawl in his words, a bit of the Old South under his clipped military tone. "Where are you from?" She got the stopwatch off the wall and handed it to him.

"Military brat. I'm from everywhere. But Mom and Dad are from Mississippi. I went to school around Boston, but I guess I didn't lose their accent."

"Boston? Did you got to Harvard?"

"MIT. Did Naval ROTC there."

She rolled her eyes at him. "Nerd. Nerds get punished around here."

"I'm also a geek."

"Do you read?"

"All the time. Especially since recovering from the surgery. Big, thick non-fiction books. Biographies of dead military leaders. Fat ones."

"Fat books or fat military leaders?"

Lance started to say something but she interrupted. "Forget it. Bend over, bookworm."

He did as ordered and Nora picked up the solid red riding crop, the one with the steel spine. She could wield it like a cane and strike him with the length of it. That would be too easy, though. The tip of the riding crop was a divided piece of leather, four inches long and forked like a snake tongue. She'd yet to find anything that stung quite as much as this particular crop did.

"You picked the number fifty earlier so we'll let it do double-duty. You survive fifty hits of this bitch, and I might even let you come twice tonight."

"You spoil me, Mistress."

She brought the viper-tongued crop tip down onto the back of his thigh. "Count for me."

"One."

"Hurts more than it looks like it would, doesn't it?"

"Fuck yes, Mistress."

"You're welcome. Keep counting."

By twenty, Lance's voice had started to break. By forty, Nora started to feel a little sorry for him. But they were only ten away. The *fifty* sounded choked, like it took every ounce of energy and every scrap of masculine pride to get that number out.

"Good man..." she purred as she ran her hand over his burning skin. "Very good."

"Thank you, Mistress. I want to please you."

"Do you?"

"Yes, Mistress."

"What's our time now?"

"Five minutes."

"Good. Bedroom. Now. Kneel facing the bed, hands on top of it, eyes closed."

She didn't have to tell him twice. Lance stood up and walked purposefully to the bedroom while Nora lingered in the dungeon gathering some bondage supplies.

When she entered the bedroom she found him doing everything as she'd instructed.

"You're so well trained. You could turn pro, sailor." She sat on the bed next to his right hand.

"Attention to detail, Mistress. Something they drill into us."

"Would you like to drill into me?"

"I'd cut off my right hand for the chance."

"Oh, don't do that. We're going to need that hand. If I get in the right mood, we're going to need all of it."

She wrapped leather bondage cuffs around his wrists and buckled them. God damn, that man looked good in leather. The cuffs on his wrists accentuated the muscular forearms. Hitting on this guy was the smartest thing she'd done all night. Maybe she'd be smart again tomorrow...and the day after...

Once she had his wrists buckled, she flung one leg over his head and moved to straddle his hands.

"Am I wearing panties? I can't remember if I put any on today." She raised her hips so he could see straight up her skirt.

"No, Mistress. You aren't."

"Good. That'll save us a step. Are you good at oral?"

"Isn't that for you to decide?"

Nora cupped his chin and traced his lips with her thumb. She picked up a snap hook and, taking his hands in hers, pulled his arms down behind his back and cuffed them together at the wrist.

"Here's your challenge," she whispered in his ear. "If you can make me come using nothing but your mouth in ten minutes or less, then I'll let you inside me next. Ready?"

"God, yes," he whispered back.

She scooted her hips to the very edge of the bed, pulled her skirt up, and spread her legs wider. She set the stopwatch again and said, "Go."

Lance leaned in and stroked her folds with his tongue. He focused on her outer and inner lips, on her vulva, taking his sweet time with her. By the time his lips enfolded her clitoris, she was almost ready to beg for it. The man might be a sub, but he knew how to tease as well as any dominant.

He continued teasing her as she'd teased him, keeping the pressure so light that it bordered on torture. But she didn't bark any orders at him. After all, if he failed to make her come in time, it was his loss as well as hers.

After a few minutes of the tease, he licked her harder and put more pressure onto her clitoris. She let herself moan, let herself pant. They were lovers tonight, not dominatrix and client. She could enjoy him as much as he enjoyed her.

And God, did she enjoy him. She enjoyed him so much that she came with a cry as her climax gripped her. As she lay panting on the bed, she heard the beeping of the stopwatch.

Slowly she sat back up on her elbows and looked down at him still sitting between her knees.

"Okay, I think we've established that you're good at oral."

"I'm glad you think so, Mistress." With a posture of sincere reverence, he kissed her thigh where her boot met bare skin.

"I didn't think you were going to get me there in ten minutes. You took your sweet time."

"You give me ten minutes with my face between your thighs, and I'll take every second of it."

She ran her hands down his arms and unsnapped his cuffs. "Are you ready for your next order?" she asked.

"Ready."

"Go to the head of the bed. Sit with your back against the headboard."

He rose off the floor and crawled across the bed. While he waited in silence she took lube and condoms out of her drawer.

"Hands up," she instructed as she knelt in front of him. She opened the wrapper and rolled the condom onto him. Whenever she fucked male submissives she always put the condom on herself. So much more fun to make him sit there and be treated like a sex slave with no control over his own body.

Once it was on, she covered him in a thin layer of lubricant. After all the pain she'd given him, she wanted nothing for him now but pleasure.

She put the lube away and dried her hands. He'd taken his sweet time making her come. She'd take her sweet time making him wait.

Finally, she straddled his thighs and gripped the headboard. Facing him on her knees she brought her mouth to his for a long, deep kiss.

"If you fuck as well as you kiss, this is going to be a good night," she said, smiling at him.

"I gave you an orgasm. It's already a good night, Mistress."

"Let's go for a great night, then." She lifted his arms and hooked his wrist cuffs through the headboard. He gripped the black steel bar with both hands.

Nora rose up and lowered herself down onto him, sinking onto his cock with a sigh of pure pleasure. She smiled as he released a ragged breath. She gripped the headboard, her hands bookending his, as he lifted his hips up and pushed into her.

"Is this position okay for you?" she asked, remembering the massive scar on his back.

"It's perfect, Mistress. You're doing most of the work anyway."

"What positions don't work for you?"

"Honestly, the only one that hurts is missionary."

"Thank God for that. I only do missionary position with missionaries."

He laughed and kissed her bare shoulder. She turned her head to the side, giving him better access to her neck and throat.

"You're a sadist for cuffing my hands," he said as he pressed his face to her hair. "I'm dying to touch you."

"I might let you if you beg a little more."

"Please let me touch you with my hands, Mistress. Please..."

"What do you want to touch?"

"All of you. Your arms, your breasts, your nipples, your thighs, your clit...every part of you I can reach. Please."

"I'll give you a choice. I can unhook your cuffs and let you touch me, but you won't get to come for another hour. Or you can stay cuffed and you can fuck me until you come. Your decision."

"I can come on my own later, Mistress. Touching you is a much higher priority."

"I can't argue with that logic, and even if I could, I wouldn't bother trying." She unhooked the cuffs and set Lance's hands free. He wasted no time and immediately ran his hands over the swell of her breasts. With eager hands he set about unfastening her corset. She helped him pull it off and it ended up on the floor by the bed. She wasn't going to waste a second folding the damn thing.

He cupped her naked breasts and sucked deeply on her nipples. Then one hand wandered between her legs and pressed against her clitoris.

As he kissed her breasts, she continued to ride him, swiveling her hips so that he rubbed against her G-spot. She held onto the headboard, steadying herself so Lance could explore her body any way he desired. His large warm hands felt so good on her, so arousing but also comforting. Strong men never scared her because strong men never harmed her. Only weak men had ever harmed her, so she knew she had nothing to fear from Lance.

Leaning back she gave him full access to her front. One hand caressed her from shoulder to shoulder, neck to breasts while the fingers of his other hand toyed with her clitoris. Soon she was panting again, desperate to come again.

"Come with me," she said. "I'm breaking my own rules. I want you to come fucking me. It's an order."

"I'd never disobey an order from you. I'll come the minute you tell me to, Mistress."

"Good, but me first."

"Always..." he breathed into her skin and the erotic tone in his voice alone nearly got her to the brink. She closed her eyes and let herself get lost in the pleasure of his hands on her body, of his cock that impaled her. So close...she felt the tension mounting in her stomach...closer...her clitoris swelled against his fingers...almost there....she heard a pounding...she felt the pounding...she inhaled and didn't exhale...and finally...

Pleasure exploded inside her as her vaginal muscles fluttered hard around him, hard enough she heard him gasping from her orgasm.

"Now," she panted and Lance needed no further orders. He came in silence but with a controlled shudder that wracked his entire body. Together they collapsed onto the bed in a tangle of arms and legs.

The sex had stopped, but she still heard the pounding. Sounded like someone banging on one of the dungeon doors. Not hers so she ignored it.

Facing Lance she gave him a quick but passionate kiss.

"Go clean up," she said, glancing down at the condom. "Bathroom's in the dungeon. We'll start round two when you get back."

"Yes, Mistress. Be right back."

He left the bedroom. Nora slowly stood and pulled the covers down on the bed. She unlaced her boots and kicked them off, wriggled out of her skirt, and unpinned her hair. But as soon as she'd stripped completely naked, the pounding in the hallway now hit her door.

"What the fuck?" She had a scarf on the door. No one would ever interrupt her with a scarf on her doorknob.

"Eleanor," came a voice through the door. "Open the door right now or I'm opening it."

Søren? Unless the club was burning down, she was going to kill the man.

"Jesus, give me a second." She grabbed a sheet off the bed and wrapped it around herself like a towel. Søren had seen her naked a million times, but she wasn't about to give him the satisfaction of seeing her naked now, not after interrupting such an intimate moment.

She threw open the door and shot Søren a murderous glare. He looked almost as disheveled as she did—his Roman collar gone, his shirt unbuttoned to the middle of his chest.

"What the hell is going on? I'm kind of busy here."

"Kingsley wants all his female employees at his townhouse now. That means you."

"Why?"

"A dominatrix was just attacked by a client."

"What? Who?"

"Mistress Natasha. She's in the hospital, Eleanor. And whoever did it got away. Now get dressed. I'll go with you and Simone to Kingsley's."

"Mistress?" She turned around and saw Lance standing in the doorway between the bedroom and the dungeon. He must have heard the commotion because he'd put his jeans back on. She saw Lance and Søren exchanging pointed glances before Søren looked back at her. She nodded her acquiescence at him.

Søren took a step back into the hallway to let her close the door. Her body, which only a few minutes ago had come alive with pleasure, had now gone numb with fear. Alone again with Lance, she gave him a look of apology.

"I have to go," Nora said to Lance. She knew Mistress Natasha and knew it would take a very dangerous—or very desperate—man to attack that woman.

"What's wrong?" Lance asked.

"Sorry, sailor," she said. "Family emergency."

Nora, Simone, and Søren headed to Kingsley's townhouse. Usually three kinksters in the back of a Rolls-Royce meant for a very pleasant car ride, but Simone had curled up with her head in Nora's lap, stunned into silence, while Nora and Søren sat quietly side by side, only their fingers touching. Søren had told her everything he knew. One of Kingsley's many minions had come banging on the doors, rousting all the official staff from whatever depraved activities they'd gotten themselves into. All they knew at this point was that a former employee of Kingsley's had been brutally assaulted during a session with a client, so it was all hands on deck.

Once at the townhouse, Søren helped Simone out of the car, but when he offered a hand to Nora, she only rolled her eyes and stepped past him.

The house crawled with submissives arriving at Kingsley's, and they all wore looks of anger and fear. It was part of Nora's job to take care of the submissives, help train them, and as the most revered member of Kingsley's staff, she considered herself responsible for the women on his payroll as much as Kingsley did. If they were going to feel safe again, she couldn't allow herself to show any weakness around them.

She put an arm around Simone's waist and, side by side, they walked into Kingsley's house, Søren behind them. Inside Kingsley's office, Nora kept her expression neutral even as the women around her wept softly or whispered back and forth to each other in hushed tones. One young submissive named Nikki grabbed Nora's hand, and Nora gave it a reassuring squeeze.

Mistress Irina rose from a chair, a look of barely controlled fury on her face. She and Nora exchanged meaningful glances—glances that said that whoever did this deed better pray the cops caught him before she and Nora did. Irina stood in the back next to Søren. Søren obviously wasn't on staff, and even more obviously, wasn't a woman, but the members of The 8th Circle considered him their spiritual leader as they considered Kingsley their earthly leader. Søren occasionally played with many of the submissives in the room but never had sex with any of them. They trusted him and often sought his advice and comfort. As far as Nora knew, theirs was the only BDSM community with its own chaplain.

Kingsley entered his office a few minutes later

with a grim look on his face. Voices exploded in questions at the sight of him, but Nora whistled hard and loud over the din.

"Quiet," she said and the women of the room went silent. No one countermanded an order from The Red Queen, Nora's Underground nickname.

"Merci," Kingsley said, nodding in Nora's direction. He stood at the edge of his desk surveying them all. "You've heard what has happened. Two weeks ago, Mistress Natasha left my employ and went to work on her own. I think many of you know her personally."

Simone nodded against Nora's shoulder. She knew Simone and Natasha were close.

"The first thing you all need to know is that she will live," Simone said. "She has a severe concussion and was unconscious when they found her. She'll likely be in the hospital several days."

"Where did they find her?" Nora asked, wanting to know all the details, wanting to know who to blame, who to punish.

"She'd been renting dungeon space at Black Forest. When Mr. Wolfe went to check on her at the end of her session, no one answered the door. He found her bleeding and unconscious on the floor. The dungeon had been destroyed. He called for help first. Then he called me."

"Did Brad see anything? Hear anything?" Nora asked, making a mental note to call Brad Wolfe herself for more details.

"Non," Kingsley said. "He was with his own

client at the time. And Mistress Natasha preferred to work alone."

Kingsley's tone was neutral but Nora sensed the bitterness lurking under the words. He had been furious when Mistress Natasha had left the fold. He hardly cared about the fifteen percent he took from each of her sessions. The money he made off his pro-dommes and pro-subs was a drop in the bucket compared to the revenue from his nightclubs. No, what infuriated him was what he considered Natasha's arrogant refusal to admit that the work she did was dangerous and required the protection of Kingsley's security detail.

"Mr. Wolfe always checked on her after each session," he said. "It's good that he did, as he possibly saved her life."

Simone's body shook with silent tears. Nora pulled her closer, held her tighter.

"Do they have any idea who did this?" Nora asked. "Did she keep a calendar or appointment book?"

"She did, but like yours, it has only initials and codes—no names. The attack might have been motivated by some sort of vengeance. The perpetrator took the time to destroy her dungeon and to leave a note behind."

Nora narrowed her eyes at Kingsley. "What did the note say?"

Kingsley sighed heavily, his handsome brow furrowing with worry. "It said, 'All the whores like her will die.'"

A collective gasp could be heard throughout the room. *Whore* was a word reserved for lovers at play in their world. A dominant man might whisper it in his lover's ear to give her an illicit thrill, but no man would dare call any of them a whore as an insult. Not unless that man wanted Kingsley on his doorstep.

"The threat might have been a ruse," Kingsley said. "Taking the time to write a note like that might simply be an attempt to cover the real motive of the crime."

"What motive?" Nora demanded. "He sounds like a psycho and we're analyzing his motives?"

"Natasha worked alone," Kingsley reminded her. "She kept large amounts of cash on her. This could be a robbery. It might not have been a client at all, but a spurned suitor seeking revenge on her alone. And yes, he could simply be a psycho, as you say, who thought he'd hired a prostitute but became enraged when she told him she wasn't."

Nora couldn't argue with that logic. She'd had a few clients who'd come to her expecting sex. They had convinced themselves that the "dominatrixes don't have sex with clients" rule was merely a cover shielding them from the law. She'd disabused a few men of the notion that a few extra hundred dollars could buy sex from her. There was only one client she'd ever slept with, and he stood in this very room.

"And there's something else," Kingsley added. "No one can find Natasha's keys. If her attacker has them, then he has keys to Mr. Wolfe's club and several of mine as well."

"Shit," Nora said, grimacing. Changing the locks wasn't an option. Members of The 8th Circle used their keys to get in and out. Kingsley couldn't change the club locks without getting new keys to over a thousand people. And that would take time. "So what now?" She asked the question that she knew was on the minds of everyone in the room. "What do we do?"

"Nothing," Kingsley said. "*Rien.* All appointments are canceled with all clients until the perpetrator is caught. I cannot police what you all do on your own, but I highly recommend you stay with friends for the time being. Safety in numbers. Don't take anyone home you don't already know and trust. If you hear anything, see anything that makes you the least uncomfortable or suspicious, you call me immediately. *Oui?*"

The women of the room nodded their understanding.

"I realize not working might cause a financial hardship for some of you. You'll all be compensated for your time off. The police believe that Natasha will likely be able to identify her attacker when she awakes."

"Someone should go to the hospital," Simone said.

"I'll go," Søren said from behind them. "You can come with me if you like."

Simone smiled her gratitude at him. Søren had

everything to lose if someone outed him as a sadist. Technically he was related to Kingsley by a long-ago marriage, and that gave him an excuse to be in Kingsley's house. But certainly, it was no excuse for being in Kingsley's club. The danger of discovery never stopped him from taking risks like this, however. One of their own had been attacked and badly hurt. Dominatrix or nun, Søren didn't care.

"Now you may go," Kingsley said. "I'll be in touch with any news as it becomes available. If any of you prefer to stay here during the crisis, you know my home is always open to you. Dismissed."

The women rose and filed out of the room. Nora overheard Nikki asking if she could stay with Irina. Tessa and Jai decided they would crash together in one of Kingsley's guest rooms. They weren't scared to go home, but they much preferred staying at Kingsley's where they could better stay abreast of what was happening.

Nora told Simone she was welcome at her house in Connecticut. Simone thanked her and said she'd think about it, but tonight she'd stay at the hospital in case Natasha woke up.

Nora watched them all go. Søren gave her a last long look before leaving the room. She smiled at him as a reassurance that she was okay. It didn't seem to convince him any more than it convinced her.

Once alone with Kingsley, she exhaled heavily and collapsed into a chair in front of his desk.

"What the fuck is going on, King?" was all she could ask.

"*Je ne sais pas.*" He put his booted foot on the chair next to her thigh. "I've spoken to the police commissioner, Detective Cooper, and everyone I know. They've all assured me that they'll do whatever they can as quickly as they can."

"Nice. Lovely. Now tell me what's really going on."

Kingsley met her eyes for a moment before glancing away. "Two weeks ago Natasha offered herself to me. I turned her down. She quit the next day."

Nora nodded, a delaying tactic while she decided how to respond. "First, can I say I'm impressed you turned her down?"

"Elle."

"Sorry. But please don't tell me you're blaming yourself for this. You have the right to say no if you don't want to fuck somebody."

"I did want to fuck her."

"So you turned her down because...?"

"The usual reason," he said. And that was all he said and all he needed to say. Three people in Kingsley's world knew he was a switch. Apparently, Mistress Natasha had sensed his proclivities, and instead of succumbing to her advances, he'd rejected her.

"It's not your fault she got hurt, Kingsley. We all get hurt around here."

"I know," he said, slipping tiredly into French. *Je sais.*

"I know you know. And I also know you know I can't cancel on my clients. That's fine for Irina and the subs. They have normal clients. My clients run the world. They're not going to be happy if I say, 'Sorry, busy,' without any notice like this."

"They'll survive a week or two without you."

"That's the problem. They will survive because they'll find a new domme. You and I have worked way too hard to build my career. This could kill it."

"It's not going to help it, *non.* But your life is more important than your career."

Nora stared him down hard. "My career is my life."

"What would you have me do? I let you keep working and *le prêtre* will kill me and lock you in a cage."

"Søren's not into cage-play."

"It won't be for erotic purposes, I promise."

Nora growled under her breath. She didn't know what to do but she knew not working wasn't an option.

"I can't let the girls think I'm spooked," she told Kingsley. "If I'm scared, they'll be terrified. I have to keep working."

"Then you'll have a bodyguard with you. *C'est ça.*"

"Bodyguard? You've got to be kidding me."

"It's either a bodyguard or no work. Your decision."

"Fucking hell...All right. Whatever. It's only until they catch the guy, right?"

"*Oui.*"

"Good. I'll call Griffin."

"Not Griffin. You two know each other too well. Far too well." He gave her a meaningful look.

"So?"

"He's a personal trainer, not a bodyguard. You need someone with experience."

"Griffin's very experienced."

"Experienced at fucking you. I'll find someone and send him to your house tomorrow. Someone you haven't slept with."

"That narrows our options."

"Elle."

"Fine. Bodyguard it is. You're the boss."

Kingsley raised a single finger and pointed it right at her.

"No fucking him," he said, his tone cold and authoritative. "No sex. No kink. This is not play-time. I'll pay his salary. You leave him alone so he can concentrate on his work."

"Like I would ever fuck some big dumb mus-cle-bound no-neck overpaid bouncer. Don't worry. Not my type."

"*Bon.* Now go home, lock your doors, get some sleep. He'll pick you up tomorrow."

She stood up and headed to the door. Before

she got there, her conscience pricked at her and she turned around.

"King, are you okay?"

He gave a very French sort of shrug. "I should never have let Natasha leave. If she'd been on my staff, if she'd been in my club..."

"She hit on you and you turned her down. She quit for her own reasons. Brad Wolfe guards those dungeons like a hawk and this happened on his watch. It could have happened on yours, too. Jesus, Natasha could have gotten mugged on the sidewalk or hit by a bus. You can't blame yourself for every bad thing that happens to every kinky person in New York."

"I can try."

"Stop being so damn Catholic. That's Søren's job."

She walked back over to him, dug her fingers into his hair, and gave it a gentle tug the way Kingsley liked. "Where's Juliette?"

"Safe," he said and that was all he said. Kingsley protected Juliette, his private secretary, as if her life meant more to him than his own. Probably because it did.

"Do you need me tonight?" Although alone in the office, she whispered the words. No one but Nora, Juliette, and Søren knew about Kingsley's secret submissive and masochistic side. She'd given a lot of herself to Lance tonight and part of her wanted to race back to the club and see if he'd stayed there. She wanted more time with Lance, but if Kingsley needed her attentions, she would give him whatever she had left and not charge him a cent for it. They fought like brother and sister most of the time, but when he needed her, she was his without question and without mercy.

"Don't tempt me," he said, closing his eyes.

"I have to," she whispered, her fingers tracing the strong line of his jaw. "It's my job."

He raised his lips to hers for a kiss. She kissed him longer and deeper than she'd intended to, but such things happened around Kingsley. He pulled back from the kiss and gave her a tired smile.

"Go home and sleep, *Maîtresse.* I'll call as soon as I hear anything."

"Oui, Monsieur." She dropped another kiss on his cheek and whispered a quick and true *"Je t'adore, mon roi"* in his ear. Kingsley had money, power and respect, but with all that came enormous responsibility. He ran a dangerous business and had the safety of all his staff weighing on his heart. Some days it was good to be the king. Days like this it sucked, and not in the fun way.

Nora caught a cab back to the club and tried to find Lance. Max, the bartender, said she saw him leave not long after Nora had skipped out with Søren and Simone. Goddammit. She wondered if she'd ever see him again, or if this craziness had scared him off for good. She hadn't gotten his last name, his phone number...nothing. He'd given her one of the best evenings of her life since leaving Søren, and now he was gone. Fuck. She could ask Kingsley for his information, but she'd feel a little pathetic and desperate trying to hunt the man down. If he wanted to see her again, he knew where to find her.

C'est la guerre, as Kingsley would say. It was for the best, anyway. She liked him and she didn't like that she liked him. *Like* led to *love* and *love* led to nasty complications. Although with Lance at least there were no foreseeable nasty complications that involved the Vatican. One more check in the plus column for that guy.

Exhausted by a night of great kink and terrible news, Nora drove home to her house in Connecticut. She stripped naked and crawled into her big, empty bed. She put her private and work cell phones on her pillow in the event Kingsley or Søren called with any updates on Natasha.

At ten the next morning she woke up and ate breakfast. Her first appointment was at noon that day, so she dressed in her kinky best. At 10:45 she heard a brisk knock on her door followed by the ringing of her doorbell and another round of knocking.

"Jesus H. Christ, I'm coming," she said as she headed to her door. She threw it open ready to chew out her new no-neck overpaid bouncer bodyguard for excessive door knocking. "Dude, seriously, holy shit."

Lance stood outside her door on her front porch wearing an awkward smile on a face made even more handsome by daylight.

"Hello, Mistress. Shall we?"

Nora remembered Kingsley's words from last night. *No sex. No kink.*

"God-fucking-dammit."

———

Ten minutes later, they were in her car heading to the city. She'd insisted on driving.

"Any reason why you lied when I mentioned Kingsley last night?" Lance asked as Nora turned south toward Manhattan.

"I've been trained to disavow all knowledge of Kingsley Edge. You get my name, rank and serial number only."

"If I had known you were Kingsley's top dominatrix, I might have checked with the boss first before going to bed with you." Lance put on a pair of dark sunglasses, which annoyed the hell out of her. First, it made it harder to read his eyes. Second, they looked so damn sexy on him she wanted to pull over and fuck him right on the side of the road.

"Under normal circumstances, he doesn't care who I sleep with."

"Maybe," Lance said, "but this hardly constitutes normal circumstances."

"Did you tell him we fucked last night?"

Lance's answer to that was to give her a look that suggested she might have just asked him the most insulting question he'd ever been asked in his life.

"So that's a no," she said.

"Yes, it's a no."

Nora groaned loudly, loud enough Lance pushed his sunglasses down to give her a *What the fuck?* look.

"Sorry," she said. "I had an amazing time last night."

"Yeah, well, so did I."

"And now you've gone and fucked it up by getting hired as my bodyguard."

"This is my fault?"

"Yes. You know King will kill us both if we sleep together while you're working as my bodyguard."

"Worse. He told me if I laid a hand on you while I'm supposed to be guarding you, I'd be fired completely—from the bodyguard job and my real job running security. And if you laid a hand on me—"

"What? He'll fire me? I don't get fired."

"No," Lance said, turning his head to gaze out the window. "He'll fire me for that, too."

Nora winced. "That man needs to be flogged. He's only doing this to piss me off."

"And maybe so I won't get distracted while I'm supposed to be protecting you?"

"Don't give him the benefit of the doubt. He's a sadist. This is the sort of shit he pulls on me. Probably payback for the time I started a rumor

Kingsley wore a toupee. He was really confused by all the women who wanted to suddenly play with his hair."

"You two have an odd relationship."

"Welcome to the Underground," Nora said. "I'm seriously going to beat the hell out of him for telling me who I can and can't fuck."

"Yeah, let's not do that. Sorry, Mistress, but I need this job. And more importantly, I need you to be safe. If some lunatic out there is stalking dominatrixes—"

"*One* dominatrix. He hurt *one* of us. Everyone's overreacting. We have no proof he's coming after any of the rest of us."

"We have no proof he isn't, either."

"Stop being rational when I'm horny," she demanded.

"I'm sorry, Mistress," he said with far more amusement than contrition.

Nora exhaled and shook her head. "Lance, if we're working together and not fucking, you have to stop calling me 'Mistress.' It's too much of a turn-on. My name is Nora," she reminded him.

"Is it?"

"It is and you know it."

"Then why did that eight feet tall blond guy call you 'Eleanor' last night?"

"He's only six-four. He only seems eight feet tall because his ego is eight feet tall."

"Who is he?"

"That's Søren, the priest I told you about."

"The best sadist in the world? That guy?"

"Him."

"He's too pretty. I don't like pretty boys."

"Don't worry. I don't think he liked you much, either." Nora tried not to smile but she couldn't help but enjoy a glimpse of Lance's possessive streak. Male subs could get very possessive of their dommes. She knew quite a few male submissive/female dominant couples that were actually monogamous. Horrifying thought.

"Why did he call you Eleanor?"

"The same reason I call him Blondie and/or Asshole sometimes—because it's annoying."

"So Eleanor isn't your real name?"

"Oh, it is. My friend Griffin told me years ago that he thought 'Eleanor' sounded too prissy. He started calling me Nor or Nora. When I became a dominatrix we used that as my domme name. Very few of the pros use their real names. Kingsley doesn't use his real last name. I don't. None of the subs do, either. Easier to keep a line between the real world and the kink world. Even *Søren* is not Søren's legal American name."

"What is his legal American name?"

Nora ran a finger over her lips as if zipping them and tossed the invisible key out the window.

"I see..." Lance said.

"Sorry. Blondie is eight feet of arrogant and annoying, but he's also pretty important to—" She almost said "me" before catching herself. "Us. The Underground, I mean. Only about three of us know his legal name, the name he pastors under. Helps keep him safe from scandal."

"A priest fucking a bunch of girls in a kink club probably should cause a scandal."

"Yes, because the people he ministers to while they're dying really care who he fucks in his free time."

"Did I just hit a sore spot?" Lance asked.

"I'm Catholic," Nora said. "The entire church is a sore spot with me. But, for the record, he doesn't fuck a bunch of girls in kink clubs. He's a sadist who plays with masochists but he never has sex with any of them."

"None of them?"

"Well..." she said. "One of them."

"Isn't that against the church's rules or something?"

"Wasn't it against the Navy's rules to have gay Navy SEALs?"

"It was."

"Did you serve with any?"

"Several."

"Were they bad SEALs?"

"No. They were excellent SEALs and honorable men."

"Would you turn them in if it was still against the rules?"

"I see where you're going with this. Look, I'm not Catholic. I don't care who he fucks as long as it's legal and consensual."

"No one should. He's the best man on earth.

He should be able to sleep with whoever he wants, get married, have kids if he wants them..."

"Do you like kids?" he asked.

"In small doses," she said. "Why?"

"No reason," Lance said and she heard a strange note in his voice. "So what's your agenda for the day?"

Nora sensed he was attempting to change the subject. She let him. "My agenda is not pissing off my clients. I see very wealthy and important men."

"Kingsley told me that."

"Yes, and they like their privacy. They aren't going to be happy to have some man they've never met before or heard of hanging around. Let me do the talking. You act mute."

"My lips are sealed, Mistress...I mean, Nora."

"Better."

"Thank you. Who's on deck?" Lance asked as they turned into a residential neighborhood.

"First up today is the Right Honorable Judge Melvin P. Bollinger."

"A judge?"

"Sixty-two years old. Foot fetishist. Absolutely adorable. He looks like a wizard when he has his robes on."

"Where are you meeting Gandalf?"

"His house. Every Saturday at noon. Standing appointment. Not literally. I sit down so he can play with my feet."

"What kind of judge is he? Retired, I guess?"

Nora turned down the judge's street. "Nope. Still active. He's some family court bigwig."

"Family court?" Lance repeated the words with some interest. "Does he—"

"Hold that thought. I have to run," she said, parking on a side street two houses down from his brownstone. She started to open the car door but Lance grabbed her arm.

"Whoa there. You can't go without me. I'm not being paid to stay in the car."

"Lance...listen to me. I have scary clients, and I have not-scary clients. Judge B. is of the not-scary variety. There are day-old kittens more threatening than he is. I'll be fine."

"I don't care. I'm going to do my job and my job is to stick by you."

"I'm in too much of a hurry to argue with you or make the obvious 'stick' joke. Come on. You can hang with Mrs. B. while I'm working." Nora walked briskly to the front door, Lance right behind her.

"That's fine," Lance said as Nora rang the bell. "Wait...Mrs. B.?"

The door opened before Nora could answer. A sweet older lady in an apron greeted her with a kiss on the cheek.

"Hi, Mrs. B. I'm sorry if I'm late. Rough weekend."

"It's fine, dear," she said. "We aren't doing anything special today. Who's your friend?"

"This is Lance. Be nice to him. He's a veteran," she said in a stage whisper and Mrs. B. gave Lance an approving look. "He's babysitting me today. Would you mind babysitting him while I'm upstairs with the judge?"

"What branch of the service, young man?" Mrs. B. asked Lance.

"The Navy, ma'am."

"Oh, he called me 'ma'am,'" Mrs. B. said to Nora. "I like him already. He can help with my cookies any day."

Nora slapped Lance on the arm. "Go on with Mrs. B. there, seaman. Those cookies won't bake themselves."

Before Lance could protest, Nora skipped up the stairs to the guest bedroom where she and the judge always played together. Mrs. B., his wife of forty years, was one of the rare understanding types. She'd been the object of his foot fetishism from day one of their marriage. She could hardly complain about getting weekly foot rubs even if they did culminate in him ejaculating on her ankles. Not knowing any differently, the virginal new bride had assumed this was what all husbands liked to do and had gamely played along. It seemed to work as they had four children and nine grandchildren, and they were still very much in love. In the past few years, however, Mrs. B. had been stricken with bunions and arthritis and hated having her aching feet touched. Hiring Nora had been Mrs. B.'s idea, not the judge's, although the good Judge Melvin P. Bollinger hadn't put up much of a fight, especially after seeing Nora in her short skirt and her strappy stiletto heels.

She knocked on the guest bedroom door and didn't wait for an answer before entering.

"Have you missed me?" she asked as the judge gave her a kiss on the cheek.

"I have. I even got you a present, Miss Nora." Judge Bollinger squeezed her hand with avuncular affection as Nora took a seat in the large burgundy armchair. She never made the judge call her Mistress, and the *Miss Nora* rolled off his tongue so naturally, she'd never dreamt of correcting him. The judge had no desire to be dominated in the way Lance did and certainly had no interest in pain. He often described his foot fetish as a "brain itch" he needed to scratch once a week. Once scratched, it disappeared for days at a time and let him go about his life.

"It's not even my birthday," she said as she extended her leg and put her right foot on his thigh. The judge ran his hands down the top of her foot to her toes and all over her high heel. With the utmost care, he unbuckled the many straps on her elaborately laced shoes.

"I couldn't resist when I saw it in the store. Made me think of you the moment I set eyes on it. I think it's supposed to be for equestrians." The white-haired and smiling judge pulled a long velvet box out from under the chair and handed it to Nora. She opened it and found a silver ankle bracelet inside with a riding crop charm attached.

Laughing, she pulled it from the box.

"It's lovely. I adore it. Will you put it on me?" She gave the bracelet to the judge who raised her foot and kissed the top of it.

"Of course, my dear. With pleasure."

Usually, Nora would have been cautious about accepting gifts from clients. Kingsley warned all his employees that clients often engaged in transference. It didn't matter if one was a dominatrix or a submissive, a therapist or a prostitute; any woman who gave a troubled man ego-boosting attention could be rewarded with the client's unhealthy and sometimes obsessive interest. But the judge had long ago proven himself nothing more than a kind older man who loved his wife, loved his life, and simply enjoyed giving gifts to everyone who touched his heart.

As the judge played with her feet, first washing them in a basin of warm water and then giving them a long, thorough massage, Nora relaxed into the chair, closed her eyes, and thought of last night with Lance. She'd had so much fun with him it almost scared her. He'd looked strong and sexy strapped to her cross, had made her laugh and made her come—twice. She remembered his desperate labored breaths as she rode him, sounds that made her weak even now as she heard the echo of them in her ears. Men couldn't even begin to fathom how erotic those little sounds could be to a woman. They were admissions of vulnerability, of being so lost in the pleasure of the moment he couldn't control himself no matter how hard he tried. And she couldn't help but smile at the thought that the entire time he'd been going down on her, the entire time they'd been having sex, he'd been covered in her welts and bruises and had even sported a Snoopy Band-Aid on his back. Nothing could minimize his manhood or his strength. Even his submission to her added to his power. He did it so naturally and without shame or embarrassment. She'd rarely met a kinky guy completely comfortable with what he was. Søren alone had that same air of "this is me, take it or leave it" that she'd seen in Lance. But she knew Søren's sense of self was hard-won whereas Lance's seemed entirely innate.

No denying it, she wanted another night with Lance. Another week of nights. Another month of nights. She wanted to make him feel everything— pain, pleasure, candle wax, crops, and kisses on every part of him. She wanted to know his body better than he himself knew it. She wanted to take him to the limits of his endurance and let him find new strengths he didn't even know he had. And she wanted to feel him inside her again but only after he'd earned the privilege.

Nora felt something warm and wet on her feet and she smiled as she opened her eyes. Looking down at the panting judge, she asked, "Was that as good for you as it was for me, Judge?"

"Even better, my dear," he said, zipping his trousers back up.

He cleaned her feet off and with great care slid her shoes on again, careful as Prince Charming to Cinderella.

Nora gave the judge a hug goodbye after he'd given her his usual fee plus a hundred-dollar tip. She almost felt guilty charging him for the sessions. She knew women who paid good money to get a decent foot massage.

Down in the kitchen, Nora found Lance sitting at Mrs. B.'s kitchen table with a glass of milk in front of him and a plate of cookies.

"How are they?" Mrs. B asked as she wiped her hands on a towel.

"Perfect." Lance took a bite from one of the cookies. "I love them with nuts."

"So do I, but my grandchildren hate the nuts. I have to make one batch for the judge and me, and another batch for the kids."

"My daughter hates nuts in anything, too. Nuts and raisins, they might as well be poison to her the way she acts when you try to get her to eat them."

"You have a daughter?" Nora asked, coming into the kitchen. For some reason, the idea that Lance had children never occurred to her.

"I do," he said and said nothing else. "Are you ready?"

"My next appointment's about half an hour away. We should head out."

"Take cookies," Mrs. B. said. "Lord knows we don't need to eat all of them."

With a brown bag full of chocolate chip cookies, they left the judge's house and returned to her car.

"Why didn't you tell me you had a kid?" Nora asked once they were back in her car.

"Does it matter?"

"I think it matters."

"Well, let's see. We talked for all of five minutes last night before going to your dungeon and none of that conversation included you saying, 'By the way, do you have any children?'"

"Fine. By the way, do you have any children?" she asked as she headed toward East 76th Street.

"I do. One daughter, age six."

"What's her name?"

"Maya."

"Where is she?"

"With her mother."

"Why isn't she with you?"

"Because I'm working."

"You're not going to give me anything here, are you? I'm fully capable and willing to torture you to get the answers I want. You realize that, yes?"

"The situation with my ex-wife and my daughter is...let's call it *my* sore spot. A sore spot and a long story."

Nora growled in frustration. Usually, only Søren could inspire such aggravation on her part. She started to open her mouth to give him some verbal abuse but felt something vibrating in her jacket pocket. Pulling out her phone, she handed it to Lance.

"Answer that for me. It's the boss."

Lance answered and had a brief conversation, which Nora heard only one side of. A "Yes" followed by a clipped "Understood."

He handed the phone back to her and sighed.

"What's up?" she asked.

"Your next appointment's been canceled. Your client is trapped on the tarmac in Toronto. He wants to reschedule for Monday."

"Isn't that a happy coincidence?" Nora said, pulling over to park by a café. "Sounds like we have plenty of time now for a long story."

They ordered coffee and sat at a table in the corner of the café by the windows. Nora kept her coat on. A woman in a black leather bustier got more attention than she'd prefer right now.

"So what's the story with you and the kid?" She blew on her coffee as she studied Lance over the brim.

"Can I ask why you want to know?" Lance took a sip of the coffee, apparently not bothered by its temperature. Masochists. Such show-offs.

"I like you. I want to know everything about you, especially the stuff you don't want me to know."

"There might be a good reason I don't want you to know."

Nora didn't back down. "I'm not asking to meet her and audition for the role of the wicked stepmother. I just want to know about her, about you and her."

"The situation...it's not something I'm particularly proud of."

"Don't care. Do you think you're the only person at this table with a past? You realize you're talking to a dominatrix here, right?"

"Right. Good point."

"So tell me about Maya."

Lance took a deep breath.

"I can't start with Maya. I have to start with her mother, Amber. I was on a short leave eight years ago in Vermont and met this beautiful woman. Smart, sexy...love and lust at first sight. One of those whirlwind courtship things. We kept in touch after I shipped out, we got married on my very next leave. I shipped out again right after the honeymoon. Amber told me a month later I was going to be a father."

"Happy news?"

"Very happy. I had a new wife I thought I was in love with and a new baby on the way. Magic. But a few months later I had metal in my back and it's no more Navy, no more career. So I go home, and we start living together for the first time since we got married. She has Maya, I have surgeries. Once she's healed up from the delivery, and I'm healed up from the IED, I think, 'Great, we can start having sex again.' But apparently, that was not to be."

Nora narrowed her eyes at him.

"Why not?"

"Amber threw herself into motherhood. I don't know what happened but being a mom changed her. There were good changes. She adored our daughter and gave her everything, all her love and attention and affection. But it was a bad change, too."

"Because she gave your daughter all her love and attention and affection?"

"Right. Breasts were for breastfeeding only. Her body had given birth to our daughter so Amber didn't consider herself a sexual being anymore. I talked to some guys who have children and they say no sex for a long time is normal, give her a year. So I gave her a year. Then two years. I ask if we can go to couple's therapy. She says I'm obsessed with sex and it's my issue, not hers. I say that I think a married couple not having any sort of sex for two entire years is not normal. She accuses me of being an insensitive sex-obsessed pervert. I start to realize that we made a huge mistake getting married so quickly. We barely knew each other. Looking back I don't even know why she married me. The uniform? The prestige of being an officer's wife? Maybe she just wanted to be a mom and thought I'd make a good sperm donor. She might even be asexual which is fine, I mean...I just wish I'd known that before marrying her."

"That would be tough. I couldn't go a week much less two years."

"Amber never expected she'd have to deal with

an injured homebound husband. I never expected to be an injured homebound husband. And God knows I never expected my wife to lose all interest in sex."

"This sounds like a recipe for disaster," Nora said, feeling nothing but sympathy for Lance. She couldn't wrap her mind or any other part of her body around the concept of not being interested in sex. And she knew lots of women with children in the kink scene who had libidos to match her own. Then again, if Amber were asexual, being married to a man with a strong libido would be a nightmare, too.

"It was. I didn't want a divorce. I thought eventually Amber would go to a doctor, go to a therapist. Something. I tried flowers and compliments and cuddling. Everything. Nothing worked. She simply decided she would never have sex again. But Maya was, *is* the light of my life. Amber threw herself into motherhood so I threw myself into fatherhood. Pretty soon Maya was the only reason Amber and I were together. We didn't even speak unless it was about our daughter. I had to have an outlet, though. I have a strong sex drive and was going nuts in that house."

"You had an affair?"

"No. Unless you consider porn an affair."

"Depends on how much porn we're talking about."

"A lot," he said without hesitation. "I moved into the guest room-slash-office, found S&M porn, and just got lost in it. I didn't think about Amber caring. She didn't want to have sex with me. Why would she care I watched internet porn? But when she used the computer one day and found some of the stuff, she went off the deep end."

"I would think she'd prefer porn to you sleeping around."

Lance shrugged. "Me, too. Seemed harmless. She didn't think so. She kicked me out of the house—the house I'd paid for—filed for divorce and sought full custody of Maya. The judge allowed the porn into evidence. I lost custody."

"You've got to be shitting me." Nora put her empty coffee cup down so hard a tiny piece chipped off the bottom. "For porn? You weren't cheating, you weren't abusing anyone."

"If it had been normal vanilla porn, I might have at least gotten visitation. Amber's lawyer argued I was a porn addict who had abusive, violent, anti-women proclivities."

"What? Because it was kinky?"

"The sites I visited were all BDSM-related. I only watched the male submissive-women dominant stuff, but that didn't factor in. That I'd visited websites that had videos of women being whipped and play-raped killed my defense. No one even cared I'd never watched that stuff. Guilt by association."

"Son of a bitch..."

Nora knew she shouldn't be surprised. The world didn't understand anything about their community, their culture. Søren was one scandal away from excommunication. That he played only with consenting adult partners wouldn't even factor into the equation. That Lance had zero desire to hurt any woman on earth didn't factor into the equation, either. "Do you ever get to see her?"

Lance nodded. "We get to talk on the phone once a week. Twice a year I get to see her. Amber lets me see her for a couple of hours on Maya's birthday and on Christmas Eve. I don't get to take her anywhere. Amber hovers the entire time watching us. I brought her some cookies my mom had made the last time I saw her at Christmas. They had nuts in them so she refused to eat them. I didn't know she hated nuts. What kind of father doesn't know his daughter hates nuts in her cookies?"

Lance finished his coffee and set the cup down far more gently than Nora had.

"I was thinking about this while I was in the kitchen with the judge's wife. Your first client today was a family court judge. I lost custody of my daughter in family court because of kinky porn. And there's a judge who sees a dominatrix once a week. Funny, right?"

"Hilarious," she said entirely without mirth.

"I can't be mad." Lance sat back in his chair. "It's my own fault. I thought I was an honorable man. I'm the kind of man who believes that a woman should feel safer if there's a man in the room, not scared that he might try something with her. The only fistfights I've ever gotten into have been because some asshole tried something with a woman at a bar and someone needed to stand up for her. I think men exist on this earth to protect women and children. That's what we're here for. We make money to protect women and children from the elements by putting a roof over their heads and food on the table. We're supposed to be physically strong so we can stand up for a woman or a child who's in danger. We walk women to their cars at night and don't turn our backs until we see the cars start. That's what men should be. And we should never ever lay a hand on a woman or a child for any reason other than protection or affection. That was always my code, and I fucked it up."

"How?" Nora could barely speak over the knot in her throat. "By watching some kinky porn instead of having an affair?"

"By letting my daughter down. I should have put her needs over my own."

"No. That's not how it works. Your sexuality is none of your kid's business. It's not your parents' business. It's not the court's business. And when your wife cuts you off for no reason, it stopped being her business. I would have killed to have had a father like you, someone who would protect me and defend me and respect me and my mom. You're kinky. So what? You can still be an amazing dad. Saying you can't be a good father because of your sexuality is like saying gay men or lesbians can't be good parents. That's absurd."

"Absurd or not, that's how the courts ruled. And until I can afford a killer attorney, that's how it will be. Unless you have a better idea?"

Nora couldn't answer. The only ideas she had involved beating the shit out of Lance's ex-wife and the attorney who dragged Lance's private fantasies into the courtroom.

"It's not right," Nora said. "It's not fair."

"It is what it is." Lance raised his hands. "I haven't given up. I'm just regrouping before the next fight."

They finished their coffee and returned to her car.

"So who's up next?" Lance asked.

"He's the CFO of some big computer company. Pineapple, Crabapple, something fruity. I can't remember the name."

"He's kinky?"

"No, he's not actually. Not really. He's a chronic pain sufferer."

"And he sees a dominatrix? That doesn't make any sense."

"Submitting to pain causes the body to release endorphins and other natural pain-fighting hormones. I see several guys who get medicinal floggings."

He waited outside the door as Nora gave the billionaire businessman the holistic flogging of his dreams. She poured her anger and frustration at the injustice of Lance's situation out onto her client. She left with a thousand dollars more than she'd had before, but it didn't improve her mood.

Lance escorted her to the car and they headed back to Connecticut. Usually, she spent her weekends playing at Kingsley's townhouse. The most interesting kinksters of the city passed through his house on a regular basis. They'd drink, they'd talk, they'd play. One time Kingsley and Søren had even gotten into something of a dominants' duel as they put their flogging and whipping skills to the test. A little alcohol plus a lot of male egos plus far too many beautiful women watching and applauding had made for one hell of an entertaining evening. But she knew the atmosphere at Kingsley's would be subdued while everyone waited for news about Mistress Natasha and the man who had attacked her. So much injustice in the world, so much suffering. On days like this Nora almost wished she could have been one of those vanilla types she usually so disdained. A nice husband, a house in the country, maybe some cats and dogs. She could write and go for long walks, maybe do volunteer work. She knew she'd be bored out of her mind after a week with a life like that. But every now and then she did see the appeal of a life lived outside the Underground.

They reached her house and Lance escorted her all the way to the door.

"You want to come in?" she asked. "I won't

jump you. I promise we can just eat dinner and talk."

"I don't know if that's a good idea. I can't remember the last time I wanted someone as much as I want you. We both might forget to behave ourselves."

Nora leaned back against her front door. "There are other jobs, you know, even if you lose this one," she said.

"This one pays better than anything I could get right now that isn't a desk job."

"Money troubles?"

"No. I'm just saving up to buy a really good lawyer and go another round with my ex-wife."

"I'd like to go a round or two with her. She can't possibly think you're a bad dad just because you watched kinky porn. That's insane."

"No violence against women," he said, wagging his finger at her. "Not even ex-wives. But I would pay good money to see you walk up to her and tell her we had sex. Really good kinky sex."

Nora reached out and grabbed Lance by his jacket lapels.

"Please..." she said, pulling him closer. "Stay with me tonight. King won't know."

"But *I'll* know. I made him a promise I would protect you without letting anything get in the way of that. And anyway, once they catch that bastard, I won't be on guard duty anymore. We can pick up where we left off."

"Promise?" She raised her hand to his handsome face, stroked the stubble on his chin.

"On my honor as a seaman," he said, kissing the back of her hand.

She tore herself away from him and went inside her house. She didn't make it much farther than the front door, however. Once she'd closed it behind her, she waited. It took almost two whole minutes before she heard Lance's boots heading down her front porch steps. Nice to know he was as reluctant to leave her as she was reluctant to let him go.

Finally, she heard the engine starting and Lance driving away. With a heavy heart, Nora looked around her house and found its emptiness almost unbearable. No, not almost. Entirely unbearable. She needed something, someone, safety and comfort, and distraction. She needed an amazing distraction. She ran up to her bedroom and changed from her fetish-wear into more normal clothes—a plain black skirt, black sweater, stockings, and low-heeled black boots. She threw on her coat and headed out again, knowing her destination before even admitting it to herself.

Forty minutes later she arrived, parking her car where no one would see it, and its telltale SAY OUCH vanity plate.

She prayed he would be home and her prayer was answered. She knocked and he opened the door, greeting her with only a raised eyebrow and not a word.

She didn't bother with a greeting, either. She merely stepped past him and walked into his house like she owned the place.

If she couldn't have Lance, she'd have the one and only man who she wanted more than him tonight.

Søren.

"**D**on't look at me like that," Nora said as she
stepped into his kitchen.

"How am I looking at you?" Søren closed the
door behind her and locked it. She shucked off her
coat and sat on the edge of the kitchen table.

"Like you've been expecting me."

"I was expecting you. I knew you'd want to
talk about Natasha. I saw it in your eyes last night
at Kingsley's."

"Ha," she said as Søren came to her and stood
in front of her. "Shows how much you know. I
don't want to talk about Natasha."

He crossed his arms over his chest. Now late
evening, he'd abandoned his clerics for normal
clothes—black long-sleeved T-shirt, black jeans.
Even off-duty he couldn't get away from all black.
She saw a glass of wine on the kitchen counter and
smelled a fire burning in his fireplace. Briefly, she
wondered if she'd interrupted him entertaining

someone. But no, it was one glass of wine—not two —on the counter. They were alone, and she was ashamed of her relief.

"Is that so?" he asked. "Then what do you want to talk about, Eleanor?"

"Nothing," she said as she raised her mouth to him for a kiss. "Nothing at all."

Søren didn't seem to care if they talked tonight or not. She kissed him first, but he kissed her harder, deeper, and with such desperate posses-siveness she almost forgot she didn't belong to him anymore—a dangerous sort of amnesia. Nora could have stopped him with a word but the only word that passed her lips came in the form of a question.

"Bedroom?"

"Now," Søren ordered and in seconds they'd reached the top of his stairs. Once there he lifted her off the floor, and she wrapped her arms around his neck, her legs around his back. As a domina-trix, she had to be strong, all the time. Men sub-mitted to her, feared her, knelt at her feet, and worshipped her. Tonight she needed to be his, needed to submit, needed to be the one on her knees. So she'd come to Søren, the one man she gave up her power to, if only for the night.

"Hurt me," she begged and he slammed her back into the wall with bruising force. His kisses were equally bruising. He bit at her bottom lip and she tasted blood.

He let her down and the moment her feet

touched the floor his hand grabbed the back of her neck with a vicious, merciless grip. In the open doorway of his bedroom, he shoved her to her knees, exactly where she wanted to be. Impossibly strong fingers dug into her skin as she rested her forehead against his hip. She breathed through the pain, breathed through it and into it, not fighting it. She had come here tonight for the pain, for the surrender, for the chance to forget everything she didn't want to remember.

"Now," he said again and the one word constituted all the instruction she needed. She opened his pants and took him into her mouth. Even as she sucked him, licked and caressed him with her lips and tongue, he gripped her neck. She clung to the fabric of his shirt with both hands as she made herself a willing slave. She'd left him, and no matter how often he reminded her of how much she missed him, she never admitted it to him. But here and now on her knees in front of him, she admitted it to herself.

She pushed his shirt up. The muscles of his hard stomach tightened as she scratched deep, scoring his skin with her fingernails. Like many sadists she knew, he had a love for pain that manifested in borderline masochism. He'd never allow himself to be dominated but he'd take any pain she gave him during sex without complaint. Sex was at its most potent to them both when laced with that sort of fire.

He thrust his hips forward and she almost

choked on him. Søren could be gentle in the bedroom but only after he'd unleashed his sadism on her. And they'd only just begun to play this game.

Without warning, he pulled her to her feet and turned her back to him. He wrenched her skirt up, pushed her black lace underwear down, and shoved his fingers inside her from behind. Bracing herself against the doorframe, she closed her eyes and forced herself to remain perfectly still as he pried her open. She grew wet against his hand, wet enough he laughed at her body's eagerness.

"Bastard," she said under her breath but still loud enough for him to hear.

"Watch your language, Eleanor. You're never too old for me to turn you over my knee."

"Spank me all you want, just fuck me first. Please."

"Please what?"

Nora rested her forehead against her crossed arms. "Please...sir." *Sir Asshole,* she said in her head. "Please fuck me."

"I will...but you'll pay for it. Now or later?"

"Later." She knew if she let him flog her or cane her now, it would be over in minutes. Later he would be calmer, colder, and the pain would drag on and on. Bargaining for sex from Søren was as dangerous as dealing with the devil. He'd give her what she asked for but payback would be hell.

"You might regret that decision," he said into her ear. "In fact, I'll make sure of it."

He withdrew his fingers from of her and dragged her down to the floor, pushing her onto her back, and draping her ankles over his shoulders. Nora groaned as he entered her, relishing that feeling of completeness she experienced only with him. His thrusts were punishing but she didn't care. She loved the pain that was proof of his passion, loved the bruises a night with him left behind on her body.

Her body filled up with each thrust and emptied as he pulled out. Every new push into her left Nora gasping, grasping for release. With only the hardwood floor underneath her, she could cling to nothing but empty air.

Soon she fell into the rhythm of his thrusts as she opened up completely to him. He touched no part of her but her hips where he gripped her. She felt like nothing more than a hole, a sheath, a body to be used. Søren topped other women, but he never had sex with them. He beat them, broke them, and if they were very good girls he might allow them to receive his come on their backs. Only with her did he share his body; she knew it had been months since he'd had sex. She felt his need, his hunger, even his loneliness with every thrust. She took the pain because it was the only thing she could take from him. Not his love. Not anymore.

One glass of wine on the kitchen counter. What would she have felt if it had been two? Would the day come when he stopped waiting for her to come back to him? Would the night come when he took another lover finally and left her in the past? Part of her feared that night more than anything else. Another part of her wished he'd hurry up and do it already so they could both move on.

Nora didn't pay any attention to how long he stayed inside her. He didn't come, nor did he allow her to. When aroused enough he could fuck forever, but not even forever would be long enough for her.

"Clothes off," he ordered after he'd caught his breath. "End of the bed."

Nora stripped out of her sweater, bra, skirt, boots, and stockings in record time. She'd made the deal with him—sex now, pay later. Later was now. Now was later.

She waited naked at the foot of the bed breathing into herself. A luxurious languor overtook her, a heaviness. When Søren buckled cuffs around her ankles and wrists, she put up no resistance. She became lethargic, listless. Her joints felt loose as if she stood in warm water and not in the bedroom of a sadist. A dozen years of practice had brought her to the place where the threat of erotic pain caused her body to relax instead of tense.

Søren cuffed her ankles to a two-foot spreader bar, cuffed her arms over her head to the bedpost. When the first blow of the cane landed on the back of her thighs, she barely flinched.

The cane was first. Then the flogger. Cane again—the smaller one that left the vicious little welts instead of the big bruises. After that a heavier flogging. Then the belt, that unholy bitch of a leather belt.

Then nothing. Nora hung from her bonds, her muscles limp even as her body burned from the hour of pain she'd endured. When Søren unlocked her, she nearly sank onto the floor. But he caught her and laid her on the bed. For the privilege of watching him undress, she managed to open her eyes. Everyone in the Underground had seen Kingsley naked at some point or other. And quite a few had seen her naked, too. But no one but Nora got to see Søren completely naked these days except for his one and only lover—her.

He unbuttoned his jeans slowly as she lay there watching him.

"Stop being such a tease," she said, a tired smile crossing her face.

"I can't imagine to what you are referring..." he said, dropping his hands.

Nora rolled up onto her hands and knees and crawled across the bed to him.

"I am referring," she said as she took his wrists in her hands, raised his arms, and yanked his shirt off, "to the fact that you are stalling, sir. You know I'm dying here for you."

"Dying? Should I say the Last Rites?"

"I'll need them if you don't get naked and get your cock inside me soon."

"I was thinking of getting a glass of wine first."

"I hate you."

Søren gave her a sharp slap on her bottom. "You'll pay for that, too, Little One."

"Run up my tab," she said, dropping his shirt to the floor. She opened his pants all the way and stroked him. "Sex with you is worth any price I have to pay, sir."

Either her touch or her words convinced him. Either or both, she didn't care. All that mattered was that the rest of his clothes seemingly disappeared and she had him on top of her and inside her again.

Their mouths met and their tongues mingled. With each thrust into her, her hips rose to meet him. Søren grasped her wrists and pinned her hands into the bed. The tension mounted in her stomach and she begged permission to come. He granted it and her body released the tension with a hundred inner flutters of her vagina all around his incredible hardness. After coming she could completely relax. She threw her legs open as wide as possible, inviting Søren deeper into her body.

"You're mine..." he whispered in her ear. "Whether you'll admit it or not, you're still mine."

She closed her eyes and said nothing. To deny him would be a lie. To agree would be to admit defeat. It didn't matter that she still loved him, that she still missed him. She couldn't go back to him, couldn't return to her old life at his feet, obeying his orders, hiding in his shadow, living a lie and counting the days until he got caught and excommunicated.

*I am yours...*She spoke the words only inside her head.

With his mouth on her throat and his fingers clasped around her forearms, Søren came with a shudder and a soft exhalation. She closed her eyes as he poured into her.

Soon she lay across his chest, her ear over his heart. He caressed her back with gentle strokes of his hand from her neck to her hip, gentle strokes that soothed her burning skin and yet made her ache even more.

"I don't believe you," he said as she pressed a few reverent kisses onto his collarbone, into the hollow of his throat.

"Believe what?"

"That you didn't come here to talk. I know you didn't come here just for sex, as much as I might flatter myself that my body tempts you that much."

"Your body should win awards, medals even. Your body should be given honorary degrees from Ivy League schools."

"In what discipline?"

"Anatomy. Maybe even chemistry. No...art." She looked up at him and smiled. "You're a work of art."

"You can keep this up all night and I won't complain, but that won't change the fact that I know you're stalling. I want you naked."

"I am naked." She pointed at her body. "You can't get any more naked than I am right now... unless you skin me and that would just be gross and messy. I know you're a sadist but I don't think even you are into flaying."

"I can't say for sure. Never tried it."

"Practice on Kingsley. Flaying is my hard limit."

"You seem to have an aversion to answering my questions, too, Little One. Your body's naked, but your heart isn't." He flicked the tip of her nose. "Would you rather answer me or let me flay you?"

"Let me think about this for a minute."

"Eleanor Louise," Søren said in a warning tone. She could only try his patience for so long before he brought out the dreaded first and middle name warning.

"Fine." She sat up and pulled a pillow to her chest. Søren stretched out on the white sheets and waited. "But just remember, you're making me talk about this."

"I accept that. Now tell me."

Nora took a deep breath as she tried to gather her words. She trusted no one in the world as much as she trusted Søren, valued his insight more than anyone else's, cherished his counsel. But he loved her, wanted her back. To talk about Lance seemed almost too cruel.

"You know you can tell me anything."

"I don't want to hurt you...not any more than I already do."

He pulled the sheet down to display the scarlet scratch marks she'd left on his stomach. Scratches? More like welts. Or worse, claw marks. He would wear them on his body for days.

"You don't want to hurt me? How do you explain these?"

She dipped her head and kissed the welts.

"We hurt each other." Søren spoke the words softly as he brushed her long hair over her bare shoulder. "It's what we do. Hurt me. Trust that I can take it as well as I give it."

Tears pricked at her eyes, but Nora ignored them. "Life has suddenly gotten annoyingly complicated," she confessed.

"Life has a bad habit of doing that."

"That guy in my dungeon last night when you knocked on the door...I like him."

"You like him?"

"I like him. I just met him. I realize this. Then again, I fell in love with you the first second I saw you so there is a precedent for me taking these feelings seriously."

"He was half-dressed and in your dungeon. Something tells me he rather liked you, too."

Nora nodded. "He's a sub. One of those knight-in-shining-armor type subs. The 'I was born to serve and worship women' types. You should hear this guy talk—it's like something from a movie or a romance novel. He really believes in all that honor and chivalry bullshit."

"I believe I warned you a long time ago about those sorts of men."

"I know, I know. 'When one is a monster, one does well to avoid knights in shining armor.' Trust me, I don't want to lose my head over this guy. Especially since..."

"Since what?"

Nora sighed heavily and with extreme frustration. "He has a kid. A little girl. It's so unfair."

"That he has a child? It's a fairly common occurrence although I can imagine that you having feelings for someone with a small child would be—"

"Terrifying?"

"That."

She shook her head. "The kid isn't the unfair part although, yeah, it does scare me. The unfair part is that this guy, he's so good. Like genuinely good—kind and protective and noble..."

Nora spent the next half hour telling Søren everything she knew about Lance. How he'd been injured serving his country and was medically discharged from the Navy, how he'd endured three surgeries, and had been thanked for his service and his sacrifice by being cut off sexually by his now ex-wife. Nora spared no details of the drama, telling Søren about the pornography that had lost Lance custody of his daughter. Søren was a priest, after all. Watching porn was akin to a parking ticket compared to what sorts of crimes he'd heard in the confessional.

"So I'm pissed," she concluded. "Pissed at Lance for taking the bodyguard job, which means we can't sleep together again. I'm pissed at the asshole who beat up Natasha. Pissed at the universe for beating up Lance. That's my job."

She gave a groan and rolled onto her side next to Søren.

"I don't know what to do," she said, tracing the scratches on his stomach with her fingertips. "I hate feeling like this."

"Like what?" Søren covered her hand with his.

"I hate feeling. Period. I just met this guy and I actually care about him? He was really good in bed but no one's that good." She laughed but Søren didn't. He always seemed to know when her jokes weren't jokes.

"There is nothing you can do for him," Søren said. "Not unless you became a lawyer or a judge and have forgotten to tell me. You say you care about him, then care about him. Be his friend if you can't be his lover. You can't give him his daughter back but you can give him your friendship."

"Like that would do him any good."

"I treasure our friendship more than anything, even more than these nights when you come back to me. No man in his right mind would spurn your love and loyalty."

"Not if he knew what was good for him." She raised her fist and play-punched Søren in the center of his chest. He caught her hand and kissed the back of it.

"Don't do that," she said. "I have to put up with enough stupid chivalry from Lance. He even calls me a lady." She laughed as if that were the most ridiculous concept she'd ever heard.

"Does that bother you?"

Nora rolled her eyes.

"No. It doesn't bother me. It just doesn't make sense."

"What doesn't make sense?" Søren asked, a slight smile at the edge of his lips. "That he called you a lady, or that you liked it?"

Nora narrowed her eyes at him. "I'd jump you more often if you didn't make me talk to you after," she said, hating him for how well he knew her, how easily he could cut through her defenses with simply a question or two.

"Physical pain is only one of the myriad forms of sadism," he said, dragging her into his arms. "You take pain much better than you take interrogation."

"I'm going to safe out if you don't stop fucking with my psyche."

"Is that so?" He pushed her onto her back and covered her with his body.

"Yes, especially since I can think of much more enjoyable parts of me you should be fucking with instead. For example, my c—"

He kissed her before she could finish her suggestions. The kiss was passionate but not desperate, not like before. He kissed her easily, leisurely, as if tonight would be the first of an infinite number of nights together, so why hurry?

"Why aren't you mad that I have feelings for this other man?" she asked as he moved from her lips to her neck.

"Because you're here," he said, holding himself over her. "And I'm here." He bent and kissed her chest over her heart.

"Why do I feel like Lance and I were supposed to meet? Like it was destiny?"

"Destiny doesn't always play matchmaker," Søren said, caressing her lips, her chin, and nose. "Sometimes destiny plays other games with us."

Nora tried not to think about Lance for the rest of the night. The things Søren did to her until about two in the morning helped keep anyone but her priest off her mind. Still, when she snuck out before dawn, it was with Søren's words ringing in her ears.

There's nothing you can do for him...

True. She couldn't help Lance but knowing that didn't take any of the sting out of that feeling of impotence. Being a dominatrix meant men bent to her will. Why couldn't the rest of the world follow suit?

Back at home, Nora crawled into her own bed and slept for a few precious hours. Her body ached from the beatings Søren had given her but it was the ache in her heart that hurt the most. She'd known Lance all of two days and already felt that every child in the world would be blessed to have a man like him as a father. That his ex-wife and the courts judged him for what he did in private was an insult to their entire world. Kinky or not, Søren was the best priest on the planet. Why the church and the state couldn't stay out of their goddamn bedrooms was beyond her. After all, the church and the state often visited her bedroom and her dungeon. She'd lost her virginity to a priest, but Søren certainly wasn't the only member of the clergy in the Underground. She even had elected officials as her clients—congressmen, one senator, lots of lawyers, and even Judge B.

Judge B....

Nora's eyes flew open as she remembered the rest of what Søren had said to her last night.

There's nothing you can do to help him...unless you became a lawyer or judge and forgot to tell me...

No, she was no judge, but she did have a judge who worshipped the ground she walked on and the feet that walked on it. Still she couldn't think of a bigger breach of protocol than to ask a client to do her a favor—a likely illegal favor.

Kingsley would flay her himself if he found out. Then again, what Kingsley didn't know didn't hurt him...

At eleven sharp, Lance knocked on her door again.

"Are you going to come in this time?" Nora asked when she found him on her front porch looking unnecessarily handsome. She was going to have to talk to him about being less attractive.

"Can I trust you?"

"No."

"Then no." Lance took a step back on her porch.

"Wait...ask the question again. I'll get it right this time."

Lance laughed and shook his head. Instead of asking the question, he simply came inside the house. "So this is the house of a dominatrix?" he said, glancing around her living room.

"Were you expecting more whips and chains? Dungeon chic?"

"I was, actually."

Nora plopped down on her couch in her cozy living room decorated with overstuffed furniture and bookcases. "Those are all upstairs in the closet. And there's some stuff in the office, but only because I keep my toy bag in there."

"You live alone?"

Lance examined her bookcase. She wondered if they'd read any of the same books.

"I do," she said. "I'm trying to imagine who could put up with me as a roommate. Maybe Job. I'd need someone patient."

"Job?"

"The dude in the Bible with all the problems who just sat there and took it? 'The Lord giveth and the Lord taketh away—blessed be the name of the Lord'? That guy?"

"Interesting. Never had a domme quote the Bible at me before."

"Gets more interesting—my mom's a nun."

"You're kidding," he said, questioning her with his eyes. He sat down on the chair by the couch. Nora had to feel a little flattered he didn't feel safe enough to sit next to her on the sofa.

"My mother wanted to be a nun all her life. But she got knocked up with me as a teenager and that dream went out the window. But after my dad was killed—"

Lance started to say something and Nora held up her hand to stop him.

"No, we are not talking about my father today," she said and Lance nodded his reluctant acquiesce. "Once I became a legal adult, there were no impediments to Mom joining a religious order. I thought she was crazy. We'd had some rough times when I was a teenager."

"Now that doesn't surprise me one bit."

"Yeah, I put the woman through ten kinds of hell. But I thought a convent might be a little extreme. I moved back in with her for a few months hoping we could make up for some lost time. Maybe some mother-daughter bonding would change her mind about throwing her entire life away."

"Didn't work?"

Nora shrugged. "Mother and daughter did not

good roommates make. Let's just say when she found out about my lifestyle, who I was sleeping with, and what we were doing, the proverbial excrement hit the metaphorical oscillator."

"The shit hit the fan."

"With gusto. That was the last straw for Mom. The world was depraved beyond redemption and the only hope for a woman of faith to remain pure in such a wasteland was to join a convent and never venture out into the world again. So she did."

"Wow." Lance gave an impressed whistle. "Catholic priest is a sadist and the sexiest dominatrix on earth has a nun for a mother. Anything else?"

Nora smiled. "Nothing that matters."

"So..." Lance stood up again. "What's the plan for the day? You ready to go?"

"I actually don't have any clients today. Rarely see clients on Sunday unless it's an emergency."

Lance narrowed his eyes at her. "Do I want to know what constitutes a kink emergency?"

Nora laughed. "Hard to explain. For some of my clients, kink is not a choice. It's like a drug. And I don't mean that in a bad way. I'm not talking about cocaine or heroin. I mean it's a drug like, I don't know...insulin or Prozac. Our sadist priest, for example. Inflicting pain for him, it works like Lithium. He can get surly as fuck if he goes without too long. You get him a steady supply of kink—maybe once a week—and the man has the patience of the aforementioned Job. So I have a client or two who need kink like someone with asthma needs an inhaler. That's one kind of kink emergency."

"What's the other?"

"The person is rich and horny and Kingsley wants to keep him happy."

"That, I can understand. But if you don't have appointments, why am I here today?"

"Kingsley's orders. If I go out and about, he wants someone with me."

"Even when you aren't working?"

Nora didn't really have a good answer for that.

"Nora?"

She started humming.

"Kingsley didn't say I had to guard you when you weren't working, did he?"

"What was that? I didn't hear you over my humming?"

"I said—"

Nora started humming again.

"Nora."

"If I flashed you my breasts would you be shocked into forgetting this line of questioning?"

"I've already seen your breasts," Lance reminded her.

"Dammit."

"Don't get me wrong, I'm not saying that wouldn't work. I'm just saying I've already seen them."

Nora got off the couch and came to stand in

front of Lance. She pulled her T-shirt off over her head. Underneath she was wearing a red push-up bra.

"Nora, I was just—"

"Too late," she said, unhooking her bra in the front.

Lance covered her hands with his before she could finish. "I don't want to lose this job," he said.

"You think if I show you my breasts you'll fuck me right here on the floor? 'Yes' is a perfectly acceptable answer."

"I think..." Lance took a ragged breath. "If you take off any more clothing, I'll beg you to take me to your bedroom, and I'll worship your body until the world ends."

"That's a long time, sailor," Nora said, pressing closer to Lance.

"Your body deserves all the attention it can get. So please don't ask me to pay it any more attention because I will."

It was moments like this that Nora wanted to curse Søren for making it impossible for her to be completely selfish 100 percent of the time like she wanted to be. Knowing Kingsley, he would ask Lance if he and Nora slept together. Knowing Lance, he'd fess up. Lance would get fired. Nora would get a slap on the wrist.

"Fucking conscience," Nora sighed. "Always cock-blocking me."

"Pesky thing, consciences," Lance agreed.

"Yes, I would be a much happier person—"

Nora fastened her bra and bent over to scoop up her T-shirt.

"Nora, what the fuck?" Lance grabbed her by the arm so quickly she flinched.

"Jesus, what?"

"What happened to you?" He spun her around and Nora groaned.

She pulled her arm out of Lance's grasp. "Nothing. Just kink."

"Kink? That's not kink. You got the shit beat out of you. Those welts are deep. Who did this to you?" he demanded.

"Nobody you know. I wasn't mugged. I played last night."

Nora pulled her T-shirt on.

"Played with who? Vlad the Impaler?"

"He's not into impaling. Not even he is that kinky. Wait, what kind of impaling are we talking about?"

"Nora, I'm not joking. Your back is a mass of bruises."

"Yeah, so what? Take your shirt off. Show me your bruises."

"I know what my back looks like. That's not the point."

Nora crossed her arms over her chest. "I think it is the point. It's okay for me to beat the shit out of you, but I'm not allowed to submit to the same kind of pain?"

"No, it's not okay. You're a woman. You don't play that hard on women."

"Are you judging me?"

"I'm judging him."

"It was a woman," Nora lied. She raised her chin and gave Lance her coldest, most dominant stare. "What are you going to do now? Go beat up a woman on my behalf?"

"You just said, 'He's not into impaling.' Was it a man or a woman you played with?"

"I never asked. Personal question, you know."

Lance turned his back on her and sat down hard on the couch. His posture was tense, his jaw clenched with anger.

"Lance?" Nora sat down next to him. "I'm a switch. I don't tell people that. I mean, everyone in the Underground knows I used to be a sub. They think I'm an ex-sub or former sub. Kingsley calls me a 'reformed sub.'"

"Not so reformed, I guess."

Nora laughed ruefully. "Yeah, I still sub sometimes. Only with one person, though. He's special. What we were was special."

"How special?"

"Sometimes he calls me, tells me he needs me, and I go to him. I left him, but...sometimes I forget that for an hour or two. Sometimes I forget for the whole night."

"Is that what happened last night? He needed you?"

Nora grasped her hands between her knees. "No," she admitted. "I went to him. I needed him."

"For pain?"

"For...everything."

"You slept with him."

It wasn't a question, so she didn't bother answering it.

"Can't have you, right? Not until they find that asshole who knocked Natasha out. A girl's got needs." She plucked at a loose thread on the faded jeans she lived in on her days off. "You think I'm a slut?"

Lance laughed loudly, so loudly it surprised her. "I think you forgot that I was in the Navy. Once upon a Fleet Week...Well, you know."

"Oh, I know Fleet Week. Except the women in the Underground don't call it Fleet Week. We call it 'Christmas in May.'"

"Trust me, this sailor is not going to judge you for having sex with two different men in one week. You'd have to do triple that to beat my record."

"Six men in one week? You deserve a medal."

"Six women," he corrected, shooting her a dirty look. "But you get the point."

"Damn." Even Nora had to be impressed by six.

"I was young."

"I wanna be that young. Can I be that young?"

Lance rubbed his forehead and groaned a little. The groan turned into a laugh.

"I'm sorry." Lance finally at up straight again. "I didn't mean to overreact. I...I just don't like the thought of someone hurting you."

"I promise, it was consensual. It's always consensual with him. I like pain just like you do. I like sex just like you do. And just like you do, I don't like it when I'm judged for what I'm into."

"Point taken. Point very well taken." He sighed and leaned back, sinking into the couch cushions. "So you're a switch? I would never have guessed, not in a million years."

"I'm a damn good domme, aren't I?"

"You are. I can't even picture you kneeling in front of some jackass man."

"He's not a jackass. Even when I'm standing I might as well be kneeling."

"Why?"

"Because he's eight feet tall."

She gave him a wink and Lance laughed again, this time in shock. "The priest?"

"The priest," she admitted. "He was my first dominant. First lover. First everything that mattered. Don't go thinking anything sick or weird, though. I was twenty before we had sex the first time, before he beat me the first time."

"What's that old line—'Methinks the lady doth protest too much'?"

"Just stating the facts."

"I want to kill him. That's a fact."

"Get in line," Nora said. "You have a lot of competition for that privilege. Mainly from me."

"Love-hate relationship?"

"Mostly hate these days."

"Is he as much of an asshole as I hope he is?"

"No," she said with a sigh. "He's just very good at playing one when he's in the mood."

"Then why all the hate?"

Nora weighed her words. She could give Lance the usual bullshit answers. Søren was a total hard-ass as a dominant—true. He loved playing mind games—also true. He's a sadist who couldn't get aroused without causing pain or severe humiliation—very true. But still...none of those were reasons to hate him. Not for her anyway. And Lance deserved better than a half-truth or a full lie.

"Hate's like lube," she finally said. "Makes it easier to get in and get out. If it was all love with Søren, if I didn't make myself hate him, I don't think I could get out again."

Lance looked at her and, although it took all her willpower, she managed not to turn away from his intense stare. With her answer, she'd let him see a part of her soul she rarely shared with anyone, the part that still loved Søren even though she didn't want to. In the Underground, she played the part of the invincible dominatrix perfectly. Even leaving Søren had become part of her legend, her mythos. She'd defeated the dominant of dominants by leaving him and his collar behind. At the club, she and Søren treated each other like equals, like rivals. It was Sheriff Pat Garrett versus Billy the Kid down there sometimes and everyone did love an outlaw. Søren stood for law and order in the Underground. Nora caused as much playful chaos as she could. And no one knew how often Nora returned to Søren's bed by cover of darkness and slipped out again before sunrise.

Now Lance knew and knowing he knew lifted a weight off her shoulders, one she didn't know she'd been carrying.

"It's hard to pretend to be something you're not," Lance said, taking her hand in his and rubbing her palm in a manner both soothing and erotic. "The guys I served with, they thought I was old-fashioned the way I treated women. They didn't know what I really was. They wouldn't have understood."

"I understand."

They said nothing for a moment, a long moment that allowed for the temperature in the room to rise, Nora's heart to beat faster, and the hunger for each other to build. Nora leaned forward to kiss Lance, not giving a damn anymore what Kingsley had decreed. Lance didn't seem to care anymore, either. Cupping the back of Nora's head, he brought his mouth to hers. But before their lips could touch a sound like a klaxon broke the moment in half.

"Fuck..." Nora growled.

"What the hell is that?"

"My hotline. Kingsley set the ringtone to something I couldn't ignore. Now I can't figure out how to change it."

She got up and grabbed her hotline phone off the charger in the kitchen. "This better be good," she said to Kingsley, now in no mood for polite hellos.

"It's good. I promise it's very good."

Nora wrote down the information Kingsley gave her and hung up. She returned to the living room and found Lance waiting by the door, his leather jacket back on, keys in his hand.

"Kink emergency?" he asked.

"How did you guess? I'll be ready in ten."

Nora changed into her fetish-wear and this time let Lance do the driving. They valet-parked at an exclusive hotel near Gramercy Park.

"So what now?" Lance asked as they left the car. "We just walk in the front door?"

"We just walk in the front door. We look nice and vanilla." Nora had put on a black trench that covered up every inch of anything interesting on her. From the outside, she looked like any other rich Manhattanite who didn't want to get rained on. Under the coat, she looked like a cross between Bettie Page and Marlene Dietrich with a little carnival barker thrown in for shits and giggles.

They got on the elevator and headed to the seventeenth floor.

"You'll need to wait outside the room. I'll be done in an hour."

"What's on the menu today?" Lance asked as the elevator doors closed.

"Some famous actor I've never heard of," she said, checking her notes. "Wants a good beating. Kingsley says he's a total asshole who's notoriously mean to his assistants. Beating the shit out of him should be fun. I might even make him confess his sins."

"Good times. Be safe," he said when they got to the door of the hotel suite.

Nora reached under a newspaper left lying outside the door and picked up a keycard. "Don't worry. I've got this one under control."

She gave him a wink before sliding the card through the lock and slipping into the room.

She found her client sitting on the edge of the bed, shirtless and smiling. He had a good body and a vaguely familiar face.

"Kingsley tells me you're famous," she said, dropping her toy bag on the floor and tossing her coat aside.

"I am. Very famous." He leaned back resting on his hands. "Want to see my Oscar?"

"Never met a man who named his cock Oscar before."

"I meant my Academy Award."

"Oh, then no."

Her client blanched and Nora smiled. God, she did love putting the rich and famous in their place. And their place was, of course, at her feet.

"It's a big deal to get an Oscar," he protested.

"Yeah, well, I have no idea who the fuck you are and I don't give a damn about your Grammy."

"Oscar."

"And quite frankly, I don't *care* who you are.

But I hear you're an asshole who treats his assistants like shit, and I think you're probably going to have to be punished for that. Say 'Yes, Mistress' if you agree."

He swallowed hard.

"Yes, Mistress."

"Good boy. Now get naked and bend over the table. Let's find out how an Oscar-winner screams."

She quickly found out how an Oscar-winner screams. Loudly and without shame. Luckily the walls were soundproof; otherwise, she might have hotel security banging on the door. She'd learned that lesson the hard way.

After an hour, her Oscar-winner had turned into a puddle of blissed-out goo at her feet. He kissed her boots, declared his undying devotion, and begged her to let him see her again next weekend.

"I might consider it," she said. "But only if I check the newspaper and see that you've issued a public apology to your assistants."

"Done," he pledged. "I'll do it today."

"Good. Now get the fuck off my feet."

Her client pulled a bathrobe on and walked her to the door. "My new assistant is outside," he said. "He'll walk you out."

"How gallant...of your assistant."

She stepped back into the hallway and found Lance and another man waiting in the hallway.

The other man had about five inches on Lance and at least fifty pounds.

"You don't have to walk me out," Nora told the heavy. "I have my own babysitter."

"That's fine," he said. "I do have to frisk you first."

"Frisk me? I don't think so," Nora said. "You can check my bag to make sure I didn't steal any ashtrays, but the body's off-limits."

"Have to do it," the bodyguard said. "Don't want any pictures out there."

"Look, the lady said don't touch her." Lance stepped between them. "This woman's a professional. She doesn't take pictures of clients."

"I'd hardly be beating the shit out of Oscar-winners if I couldn't be trusted not to blow their covers, now could I?" Nora chided in her most patronizing voice. "I don't have a camera on me. Your boss's little secrets are safe. We're leaving."

She turned around but stopped when a big heavy hand clapped down on her shoulder with enough force to make her knees buckle.

"Excuse me—" she started to say but all words became unnecessary when Lance grabbed the bodyguard by the forearm. In seconds Lance had the man on his stomach, his arm twisted behind his back.

"You touch her again and you lose this arm," Lance said, his voice calm but menacing.

"Get the fuck off me." The bodyguard tried to rise up and Lance slammed him back down again.

"You fight like a bouncer. In other words, you're a shitty fighter. So stop trying or I'll dislocate your shoulder for the fun of it."

"That is fun," Nora agreed. "Especially when you pop it back in again."

"You ready to go, Mistress?" Lance asked.

"I was ready five minutes ago."

"Then let's go. You," Lance said to the man underneath him, "you stay here. I'll walk the lady out."

"What lady? You mean the slut in the black boots over there?"

Lance sighed. With one jerk of his arm, he popped the man's arm out of his shoulder socket. The man screamed even louder than his boss did.

"Put his shoulder back in right this second." Nora rolled her eyes.

"Anything you say, Mistress." With another jerk, he popped it back and the man screamed again.

Lance stood up and left the man on the floor writhing in pain. Arm in arm she and Lance walked toward the elevator.

The elevator doors closed and she and Lance dissolved into laughter.

"Thanks for taking care of that big dumb behemoth for me. Does he not realize 'slut' is a compliment in our world?"

"The bigger they are, the harder they fall. I probably shouldn't have dislocated his shoulder."

Nora shrugged. "Kingsley once sanded a guy who got too handsy with one of the submissives."

"Sanded? Like with sandpaper on sensitive parts of the male anatomy?" Lance winced.

"No, that would have been barbaric."

"That's a relief."

"He used an electric sander."

———

Nora and Lance swung by Kingsley's for lunch and put Mr. Oscar-Winner on the no-play list. Kingsley had a strict one-strike-and-you're-out policy for clients. One misstep and they lost any chance to play with his employees, ever. Too bad. The guy had been a decent tipper.

After lunch, they drove back to her house in Westport where Nora changed back into normal clothes again.

"I hope that wasn't a total waste of an afternoon," Lance said as she returned to the living room back in her jeans and T-shirt. She got two beers out of her fridge—Achel Extra Blonde—and handed one to Lance. She kept the other for herself.

"And milady's a beer drinker, too," Lance said with a heavy wistful sigh.

"Only rare European beers brewed by monks," she said. "Friend of mine made me try it while we were in Belgium."

"Good stuff," Lance said, after taking a long drink.

"Thanks for taking care of that asshole today. I don't like admitting this, but he did scare me."

"Scared me, too," Lance admitted.

"You put him on his face and dislocated his shoulder."

"He could have done the same to me if he knew what he was doing."

"I'm still impressed."

"Dick-swinging bravado impresses you?"

Nora smiled at him. "Acting strong even when afraid impresses me. It's not courage if you're not scared." She leaned forward and they clinked their beer bottles together.

"I'm just glad you're safe. That's all that matters."

"You were with me. Of course I'm okay."

Lance leaned forward to set his beer on the coffee table. Nora lifted the back of his shirt.

"Hey, you, what are you doing?" he asked, looking back over his shoulder.

"Relax. I like seeing the souvenirs. My clients rarely book back-to-back sessions with me. I never get to see the aftermath."

Lance grabbed the back of his shirt and yanked. He bent forward and let her have full access to his back.

"Damn. I do good work. You still have some nice bruises. Want me to get the mouthwash?"

"Mouthwash?"

"Little trick Kingsley taught me. Applying mouthwash to bruises makes them fade faster. They'll be gone in two days if you want."

"I think I'll keep them," he said. "You're keeping yours, aren't you?"

"I always keep mine," she confessed. "You like your bruises?"

"I love them. They're a turn-on."

Nora traced a few of the red welts with her fingertips. Lance closed his eyes and inhaled.

"Next time I'll leave some marks on the front of your body," Nora said into his ear. "On your hips...your stomach...front of your thighs...I'll make sure you can see them. Would you like that?"

"Yes, Mistress," he whispered.

"Do you get aroused when you look at the welts and bruises the day after a scene?"

"Yes."

"Do you masturbate the day after when you look at them?"

"Every day until they heal completely."

"Wish I could watch that."

"I'd love for you to watch me."

Nora could feel the muscles in his back tensing under her touch. "Do it for me now."

"Nora, you know I can't."

"Oh, I think we both know you can. And I think we both know you want to. Kingsley said no sex. He said nothing about masturbation."

"We're splitting hairs a little."

"I have turned finding loopholes in rules into a high art. If it were an Olympic sport I'd medal in it. And don't pretend you don't want to. You know you want to come for me while I watch. I know you want to show me how much our night together turned you on."

"God, yes..."

"I'm not ordering you to do it because that would be kinky. King said no sex, no kink. We're not going to have sex. We're not going to do kink. We're just going to hang out on the couch. And if the spirit moves you...then it moves you."

The spirit moved him.

Nora turned sideways and leaned back against the sofa arm. She got nice and comfy as Lance faced her on the couch, a look of desire shining in his dark blue eyes.

He scooted down so that he was half laying on the couch, half sitting, the sofa arm as his pillow. On the extra-long sofa, their feet barely touched.

Lance unbuttoned his jeans and slowly pulled down the zipper.

"You men are such fucking teases," Nora said, shaking her head. Lance was as bad as Søren.

"Give me some time. I might be shy."

"The man who was naked on the floor of my dungeon with his wrists cuffed behind his back and his face buried in my pussy is shy?"

"I said I *might* be shy. I didn't say I *was* shy."

"Tease," she repeated.

"Guilty."

He pulled his erection from his pants and slowly started to stroke himself. "I'm so going to get fired for this," Lance sighed.

"Don't worry about it. If Kingsley asked if we had sex the answer is an honest 'no.' If asked if we did kink, the answer is..."

"No."

"Good boy. I mean...right answer."

"Thank you. I did go to MIT. I should be able to answer simple yes and no questions even with a painful erection."

"It might be painful but it's sexy as hell. You have a gorgeous cock," Nora said with an approving nod.

"Thank you, I think."

"You're welcome. I'm a cock connoisseur."

Lance's head fell back as he made another pass down and up again. "What makes a cock gorgeous?"

"Hmm..." Nora tapped her chin. "Good size. Too big looks comical. Too small is, well, a bit disappointing. Although what women consider small and what men consider small is very different. We're much more into girth than length, and you have very impressive girth."

"Is that so?"

"Definitely. A pencil might be nine inches long, but you don't want a pencil poking your cervix."

"Good point."

Nora bit back a laugh. "I can't believe you

made a pun while jacking off on my couch. Remind me to kill Kingsley the next time I see him. I want to fuck you so much right now it hurts."

"That much?"

"I really like puns."

Lance stroked again and Nora couldn't stop staring at his hardening inches, at his roaming hand, at the veins in his strong arms, the flat plane of his stomach.

"I really like *you*," Lance said, smiling through half-closed eyes.

"I like you, too," she said, watching as his fingers teased the head. What she wouldn't give to roll forward and lick that little drop of semen off the tip just to make him moan. "More than I want to."

"You don't want to like me?"

"Not as much as I do, no. I'm not one of those angst-ridden types who constantly worries about whether or not she's doing the right thing, making the right choices or God forbid, pissing someone off. I piss off more people before 10 a.m. than most people do all day."

"Good for you. That takes effort."

"I'm a natural. But to be like me, to do the job I do, live the life I live...I need it to be complication-free. You, Lance, are a complication."

"I'm a complication?"

"You could be. I'm a dominatrix. So I'm not a prostitute, but let's not quibble. I work in the sex trade. My clients don't get to fuck me, but the kink is their version of sex. They take their clothes off, I whip their testicles, they come all over my nice rug which I have to get cleaned five times a week."

"You might have to get your couch cleaned after I'm done," he said with a wink.

"It's my couch. Trust me, it's Scotch-guarded. Keep rubbing."

"I'm rubbing. So you're a dominatrix. I can live with that. Any other problems?"

"No problems." She shook her head. "I said complications, not problems. A few of the professional dominatrixes I know end up dating clients. There's a lot of heat in those sessions. Husbands and boyfriends aren't thrilled at the idea of having a wife or a girlfriend who spends a lot of time alone with naked, horny, kinky men."

"I can see how that would be a complication. I can handle it, though."

"Can you handle these?" She pointed to her back. "I'm a switch, remember? You're not. If and when I need or want pain or domination, I couldn't get that from you, right?"

"I can't hit a woman," he said. "Not for love or money."

Nora nodded. "Thought so. So that means when my switch-side comes out, and trust me, it comes out, I'd take it elsewhere."

Lance wrapped his hand around his cock. Nora had never wanted to be a man's right hand so much in her life.

"I could live with that. I wouldn't like it...but as long as it didn't happen all the time."

"About once every couple of months, he calls me and I go to him."

Lance seemed to think about that. "Once every couple of months is tolerable."

"This might not be—I don't want kids," she said, giving him a "take that" stare.

"I already have a kid," Lance countered.

"I don't want to get married," Nora shot back.

"I've already been married." Lance raised his eyebrow in a two-can-play-this-game taunt.

"You keep this up and I'm going to start masturbating on the couch, too."

"Was that supposed to be a threat?"

"It was," Nora said with a sigh. "I think I need to work on my threatening skills."

"I think I need to come."

"I think you need to come too as much as I need to watch you come." Nora rolled up onto her knees and scooted closer to Lance. "Will you come for me? Just a request, not an order."

"Since you asked so nicely..." He turned his head and smiled at her, a lazy, sexy, seductive smile with a glinting twinkle in his eyes that made her feel like she'd just eased into a hot bath. And like a woman soaking in a hot bath, she was undeniably wet.

"I wish I could help," she said as his hand started to move faster.

"You are helping. Just being around you makes me hard."

"I know I'm cute but that's quite a compliment."

"It's not the way you look," he said, his voice getting breathless. She raised her eyebrow at him. "Okay, not entirely. The world is full of beautiful women, but there are so few of them like you."

"And what am I like?"

"You're like a queen. You're strong and fearless. Men serve you. They want to serve you. Hell, they should serve you. You don't answer to anybody. You don't apologize to anyone. You walked into that judge's house like you owned it. You beat the shit out of a billionaire. You put the moves on me faster, harder, and smoother than any soldier, sailor, or Marine ever put on any girl in any bar in the history of the world. You make me wish we lived a thousand years ago. I'd slay dragons for you, Mistress."

"I like dragons."

"Then I'd tame one and bring it to you as tribute, complete with collar."

"Do you want to wear my collar, Lance?" Nora asked, the question coming out before she even realized what she was saying.

"I'd wear it with pride, Mistress. Every night of my life."

Nora reached out and laid a hand on his neck, pressing lightly into his throat, making a collar out of her fingers. Lance closed his eyes, let his head fall back.

"Are you fantasizing?" Nora asked, pulsing her hand against his neck.

"Yes and no. It's just images right now."

"Tell me."

"You...naked."

"Good image."

"And on top of me. I love being tied down," Lance confessed, his hand moving faster on himself.

"You look amazing in leather wrist and ankle cuffs. I bet with your body you'd look incredible in a black leather chest harness. Maybe some arm-bands for those amazing biceps of yours."

"I'm fantasizing about you fucking me, and you're fantasizing about dressing me up?"

"It's a girl thing. You have a great body. I'd love to show it off to the world. Or at least my kinky little corner of it."

"Gorgeous body? You've forgotten the scars."

"Scars are sexy. Scars mean you've lived."

Nora felt Lance's pulse beating against her hand, growing harder every second. "What else do you see, Lance?"

He opened his eyes and looked at her. "A future with you. Maybe."

Nora swallowed and whispered, "Big maybe. Now come for me."

With a soft gasp, he came, semen shooting out and landing on his stomach.

"God, I needed that," he said, his body relaxing deep into the couch.

"I could tell."

"And I think I need a tissue. Maybe three..." He glanced down at the semen decorating his stomach and laughed. She adored him for the laugh because it meant he had no shame, no embarrassment about his body, about his sexuality. Many of her submissive clients were ashamed, embarrassed, and scared to come out of the closet. Not Lance. Not at all.

"Let me," she said, dipping her head. With a quick flick of her tongue she lapped up a small patch of semen. Lance groaned as he slid a hand into her hair.

"You're a sadist, Mistress Nora."

She looked up at him with a wicked grin on her face. "You're like the perfect male submissive. How did that happen? I want twelve of you."

Lance gave her a half-smile. "I have this drive to be perfect at things," he said. "Always have. I was the five-year-old kid who made Lego houses you could live in. I wanted to be the perfect Navy SEAL, and I was until I got wounded. I tried to be the perfect husband and then the perfect father. That blew up in my face. Now, at least I can be the perfect sub. With you anyway. With you and for you, Mistress."

Nora grabbed a box of tissues off the end table.

"Here. Clean up. We'll go get some lunch or something. If we don't get you out of this house soon, I won't be held accountable for the things I do to you."

She slid across him and headed to her bathroom. Halfway there she heard the klaxon tone of her hotline phone blaring from her kitchen. She took a detour and grabbed the phone.

"King?" Nora asked as she answered the phone. "Any news?"

"Bad news first."

"What's the bad news?"

"The man who attacked Natasha?"

"What about him?"

"Elle...he broke into your dungeon."

"What? He was in my dungeon?" Nora demanded.

"That's also the good news."

"Please tell me someone caught him in the act."

"Let's just say you owe our friend Griffin Fiske a debt of gratitude. I can guess in what form he'll take repayment."

"Griffin?"

"I underestimated Griffin. He'd make an excellent bodyguard. I should apologize to the man."

"How bad is it?"

"Let's just say you're going to need a new rug, *Maîtresse*. Yours is...bloody. And the culprit is in the hospital."

Nora listened for a few minutes as Kingsley told her the story. They hung up and Nora returned to the living room and found Lance picking his shirt up off the floor.

"You're not going to need that," she said, nodding at the shirt in his hands.

"Why not?"

"They caught him. And by 'they,' I mean my friend Griffin caught him breaking into my dungeon. Griffin beat the shit out of the guy."

"Thank God you weren't there." Lance sounded genuinely relieved.

"I know. I wouldn't have been nearly as merciful as Griffin. I would have killed him and then gotten arrested. Again. If he laid a finger on my red-and-black riding crop, I swear to God I'll rip his heart out."

"This is the guy who beat up Mistress Natasha? They're sure?"

"Natasha came to a couple of hours ago. She knew the guy—a client of hers with money trouble. King was right. Just a robbery. He got five-thousand dollars off Natasha. Decided to see if the other dominatrixes in the city also kept cash on them. Has a nasty drug problem apparently. Owed a lot of money."

"I want to beat the shit out of him, too. Why does this Griffin guy get to have all the fun?"

"Speaking of having all the fun...you know what this means, right?"

"Tell me," Lance said, a smiling forming on his lips.

"You're not my bodyguard anymore."

Lance let his shirt drop from his fingers. This time he didn't bother to fold the damn thing.

"Good boy."

Lance followed her up the stairs. The second he stepped into her bedroom, Nora shoved him hard against the wall and kissed him with everything in her.

"This is what's going to happen," she said, between soft bites of his lips. "I'm going to cuff you to my bed. Then I'm going to decorate the front of your body with a set of welts and bruises to match the set on your back. And then I'm going to climb on your cock and ride it until it breaks off. You have any objections to that plan?"

"Only the part about my cock breaking off, Mistress." He started to reach for her but Nora caught his hands and pressed them into the wall.

"That was erotic hyperbole."

"Then no, I have no objections."

"Good. Not that I would have changed my plans if you did. You're mine today."

"All yours. Every part of me."

Nora's heart clenched at the solemn tone of his pledge. If only she could believe that, if only she could keep him. Then again...maybe he meant it. Maybe she could keep him. Maybe she would keep him.

"Get rid of the clothes. Pull the covers back. Lay in the center of the bed. Say hello to my ceiling. Now." She snapped her fingers and Lance immediately unzipped his pants. He'd just come a few minutes ago but she could see that he was already getting aroused again.

As Lance moved to follow her orders—naked, covers back, center of bed, hello ceiling—Nora threw open her closet and dug for supplies. Playing on the front of the body required a bit more finesse than the back did. With the thicker skin on the back of the body, one had to work very hard to do real damage back there. But the front of the body had all those pesky internal organs to deal with.

Nora found her smallest, thinnest cane—a white plastic little beauty no bigger than a conductor's baton. She also found her smallest flogger with the thin, sharp tails. She didn't know if Lance liked CBT or not. Guess she'd find out.

"Comfortable there?" she asked, emerging from her closet with all the necessary supplies.

"I want to die in this bed." Lance stretched out, luxuriating on her black sheets. Goddamn, the man should be legally required to be naked constantly.

"I'm not into necrophilia," Nora said.

"I want to live in this bed."

"Better," she said as she opened the side table drawer. She pushed aside her vibrator collection and dug until she found the wrist and ankle cuffs she kept in a box. "Keep enjoying the bed. I'm not planning on letting you out of it for a few hours."

"Can't think of any better way to spend a Sunday."

"Helluva a lot better than church anyway. Now give me your wrist."

She cuffed both wrists and both ankles before hooking them to spreader bars. With twine she tied his wrists and ankles to each corner of her bed.

"How do you feel?" she asked once she had him tied down and immobilized.

"Exposed. Vulnerable."

"Good. You okay with spread-eagle?"

"I am. Haven't been in it in a while. You might want to uncuff the ankles before the cock-riding, though. Might need some traction."

"If you're good, I'll consider it."

"Mistress, I want to be nothing but good to you."

Nora pulled her T-shirt and jeans off and wearing nothing but her red lace bra and panties, climbed onto the bed.

Lance's body had been denied to her for only two days, but it was with hungry hands that she touched him, stroking his body from neck to knees.

"So you're okay with heavy bondage?" Nora caressed his exposed inner thighs, lightly tickling them with her fingertips.

"I haven't done it in a long time, not since college, but I have no problems with it."

"Yes, you mentioned you were a boy-toy for one of your professors. How did that happen, anyway?" She tickled behind his knee and Lance flinched. She'd tied him down so thoroughly he couldn't pull away from her touch. Good.

"It just...happened." Lance shook his head and

smiled. "My first semester freshman year I got a job on campus as a professor's assistant. She taught economics, something I never planned on taking. Actually I never took any e-con courses. I didn't ever want her to have second thoughts about sleeping with a student. I practically lived in her house, but never stepped foot in her classroom. I didn't want to get her in trouble."

"I understand," Nora said, teasing Lance's testicles with the flogger. She didn't hit him with it, merely let it tickle him with the tips of the tails. "I met Søren when I was fifteen. Love at first sight with a Catholic priest. I lived in fear for years that we'd get caught."

"You mean you lived in fear that *he'd* get caught. You weren't the one who took the vow of celibacy."

"Still..." she said, brushing the little flogger over his hips and thighs. "I know the feeling. That feeling that what you're doing is right, so unbelievably right, and yet knowing the entire world would say it was wrong...Terrifying to think someone would try to take a love like that away from you."

Lance nodded his understanding. "She, Katherine, was amazing. I didn't care she was almost twenty years older than me. She was smarter and sexier than any of the girls on campus my age. Somehow she just knew what I was, what I needed. And God, she gave it to me. Pain, bondage, discipline... Being in the Navy was a vacation compared to the discipline she imposed on me. At least the Navy never told me I couldn't have an orgasm for ten straight days in a row."

"Vicious woman. I love her already."

Nora grabbed the tips of the flogger tails and struck Lance's inner thigh.

"I did, too," he said. "She'd order me to go two weeks without coming and then the week after she'd make me come as much as humanly possible. Zero to sixty. I'm not kidding there. I went from having zero orgasms in two weeks to having sixty orgasms in two weeks.

"I just tried to do the math on that to see how many orgasms a day that was and both my brain and my vagina started hurting."

"Comes to four-point-two-eight orgasms a day."

"How do you have point-two-eight orgasms?" Nora furrowed her brow at him.

"Very carefully..."

Nora stopped her flogging long enough to laugh.

"Don't do that," she warned Lance. "I'm going for light CBT here. You make me laugh, and it's going to fuck up my aim."

She took a quick breath before striking at the base of his penis. Lance flinched but didn't cry out or safe out. Clearly his professor/dominatrix had introduced him to cock-and-ball torture as well as orgasm denial back in their days together.

"Good?" she asked.

"Hurts like hell. Love it."

"Men get a little jumpy when you get your floggers near their cocks. Of course, I have a few clients who can't even get it up until you beat their junk into the ground."

"That might be a hard limit for me. But as long as you go easy, the flogging actually helps with the arousal. Nothing like a little cock-flogging to get the blood to all the right places."

The blood was certainly pooling in all the right places. Lance was rock hard and Nora had to remind herself she'd promised him a good beating before the sex. Next time she'd fuck first and give beatings later.

Nora peppered Lance's erection with a few more lashes of her flogger. Just enough to get him panting and wincing. One final blow sent him breathing through his clenched teeth.

"That hurt?" she asked.

"Oh, hell, yes."

"You're welcome."

Nora tossed the flogger to the floor and without giving Lance any warning, she brought her mouth down onto him. He gasped and Nora almost laughed again, would have laughed except she had her mouth full at the moment.

"Oh, my fucking God..." he breathed as Nora licked him from base to tip before grinning up at him.

"That's the spirit. Oh, and don't you dare come, by the way. I won't make you wait two weeks, but you don't get any more orgasms until I've had two. At least two."

"I'm good, I promise. You could suck me off for an hour and I wouldn't come."

"I'm not going to suck you off for an hour."

"You can't blame me for trying."

"Nope, but I can punish you." Nora got out her cane and flicked Lance hard with it right on his hipbone. He grunted in pain.

"Ouch," he said after taking a deep breath. "Fucking ouch."

"Say 'ouch' again. You know that's my favorite word..." Nora flicked him in the same spot and Lance's hips scooted two inches over on the bed. He could scoot but he couldn't hide.

Again and again, she struck him along the thin sensitive skin of his hips and inner thighs. She had to give the man credit. He took the pain like a pro and never once begged for mercy.

"I'm loving these bright red marks all over your hips," Nora said, admiring her own handi-work. "I've seen tabby cats with fewer markings."

"Nice symmetry." Lance raised his head and looked at the red stripes that decorated him from knees to chest. "I like the V-patterns."

"One of my trademarks. Some Mistresses just go for the kill—brute force is their game. I like a little finesse, a little artistry."

"A little fucking?" Lance prompted.

"Oh, if you insist."

"Only if you think I've earned it, Mistress."

Nora leaned over him again and brought her mouth to his. "I think you've earned it."

She let her lips hover an inch over his, high enough that he had to raise his head to kiss her. She pulled back another inch and he raised his head another inch.

Once more she pulled back this time out of reach.

"Please, Mistress..." All the playfulness, the teasing had gone out of Lance's voice. She heard only desire.

"Please what?"

She expected him to say *Please kiss me* or *Please fuck me*. Either wish would have been immediately granted.

Instead, in a voice low and hungry he whispered, "Please make love to me."

Nora didn't have a snappy comeback for that. She had no words at all. All she could do was look at him, at this man beneath her who'd put himself into her hands, had given her his body to be used any way she desired. The submissive existed to offer himself at the feet of the domme. So why did she suddenly feel so humbled?

Closing her eyes, she kissed him again, kissed him with renewed passion, renewed determination to make all his deepest fantasies come true.

She kissed her way down his body, pausing for a few minutes to tease his cock with her tongue again, before making her way to his ankles. She unstrapped him from the spreader bar so he could have all the traction he needed. Her hands roamed all over him, taking in every inch of his warm, hard body. She didn't know why she couldn't stop touching him. Something in the back of her mind told her to enjoy him while she could. That made no sense, however. She had him tied down to her bed. Where could he possibly go?

"Please..." Lance begged again and Nora raised a finger to her lips.

"I will," she said. "But I want to enjoy your body now."

"It belongs to you. Enjoy it any way you want."

She bit his quivering stomach, nibbled the insides of his arms all the way to his wrists. She traced his collarbone with her fingertips, massaged his chiseled thighs.

Before she knew what she was doing or why, Nora put both her hands on Lance's face. From his face, her hands moved down his neck and up both arms. She ran her hands over his chest, his hips, his legs, and over his feet. Søren had done this to her so many times she lost count in their years together—touched her like this. *I own you,* was the message. *I own every part of you.*

She said nothing while she touched him, claimed him, and he said nothing, either, perhaps recognizing the significance of the moment. Finally, she couldn't wait anymore. She took a condom from her drawer and rolled it onto him. She took off her underwear and straddled him.

With her mouth on his mouth, she took him in her hand and guided him inside her.

At first she barely moved, wanting nothing more than to take him into her and let him fill her. She brought her breasts to his mouth and let him suck deeply on her nipples while she moved gently against him.

She slid up and down his length, going as slowly as she could, not wanting to rush the moment. With her hands on his chest, she held her upper body steady as she made slow ovals with her hips, lightly grinding her clitoris against him.

"You feel amazing inside me," she said, bending to kiss his chest.

"I do feel amazing inside you."

"Smart-ass." She sat up and scratched his chest and stomach lightly with her fingernails, light enough his skin shivered under her hand.

"I'm only telling the truth. I want to stay inside you forever, Mistress."

"I might just let you."

She braced herself against the headboard and started to move faster on him.

"Don't come," she ordered as she rode him harder, feeling her own orgasm starting to build.

"No, ma'am. No chance."

"Good." She didn't want this to end yet. She didn't want it to end...ever.

The pressure rose in her back and stomach. She dug her hands into Lance's biceps so hard she knew he'd have bruises. He didn't raise any objections. Instead he lay beneath her whispering erotic encouragements to her.

"Use me, Mistress…"

She used him. She used him to climax hard, hard enough Lance seemed to feel it. He closed his eyes tight as she cried out with intense pleasure, every muscle in her stomach spasming.

She collapsed onto his chest and breathed, moving just enough to keep him hard.

"I'm not done," she said.

"I know you aren't."

"I just need a minute."

"Take all the time you need."

After she caught her breath she kissed him again. His tongue slipped between her lips and she lightly bit it. The sexy sounds he made while their tongues intermingled and the presence of him still inside her and still hard made her eager for another round. She pushed against him, her body alive with want and hunger.

"Come with me," she said and Lance's only response was to dig his heels into the bed and thrust up and into her. The room filled with the sounds of their need for each other. The bed creaked underneath them. When Nora came again she felt as if she rose so high her breath could fog the ceiling. As soon as her orgasm peaked she reached out and quickly freed Lance's hands from the wrist cuffs. He rolled up and wrapped his arms around her, buried his face against her breasts, and came hard, clinging to her.

After they both came, Lance wouldn't let her go. He held her close, held her tight, and said nothing. He lay back on the bed and brought her down with him. Exhausted and spent she fell asleep on his chest almost immediately. He was still inside her.

Nora woke up a few minutes later. Or maybe it was an hour. Who knew? She didn't know and didn't care. All she knew was that Lance lay next to her in bed where he belonged. She bent her head to kiss him but paused when she heard a sound.

Someone was at her door.

Lance stirred and she kissed him.

"Stay here," she whispered. "Sleep. It's an order."

He flipped over in her bed and fell back to sleep. Poor thing, she'd worn him out. Nora found her grey silk bathrobe and knotted it around her waist. She walked downstairs and without looking out the window, she opened the front door.

"It's Sunday," she said. "Isn't this the one day of the week you have to work?"

"You know I always take the afternoon off between Masses," Søren said. "How are you?"

"I'm fine," she said to Søren who stood on her porch wearing jeans, his black leather motorcycle jacket, and holding his helmet in his hand. "I wasn't even there when that guy broke in."

"I know," Søren said.

"So you're here because...?"

"Do I need a reason?"

"I broke up with you, so yes, you do need a reason."

"You were in my bed last night."

"I'm in my own bed today," she said.

Søren looked over her shoulder. Nora closed her eyes and winced. She knew exactly what Søren was seeing. Two open beers on the coffee table.

"You still drink Achel Blonde," Søren said.

"It's good stuff," she said.

"I know," he said. "I'm the one who introduced you to it."

He met her eyes and Nora refused to look away.

"You should go," she said. "If someone sees you here..."

"Of course," he said, his tone even. "I see that you're safe. That's all I needed to see. I'll leave you to your guest."

He turned to leave and Nora stepped out onto the porch. "Søren?"

"Eleanor, it's forty degrees out. Put on shoes if you're going to stand outside."

"I'm an adult," she reminded him. "I'm not fifteen anymore."

"An adult would wear shoes in forty-degree weather."

She stared at him and shook her head. "You..."

she said. "You are infuriating."

"Me? Because I don't want you getting frostbite?"

"Because you will not move on."

"I will when you do," Søren said. "And don't pretend you've moved on simply because you're sleeping with someone else tonight. My house-keeper comes tomorrow. I have to change the sheets before she cleans my bedroom. There are stains on them. Yours and mine. I haven't had to do that since the last time you spent the night with me."

"Last time you called me and asked me to come to you."

"And you came when I called. You came several times if I remember correctly, and I always remember correctly."

"That was just sex."

"Say that again. I might believe you."

"It. Was. Just. Sex."

He raised his chin and looked down at her. With his eyes narrowed he said softly, "No...still don't believe you."

"Find someone else to fuck," Nora said.

"Find someone else to fuck?" he repeated. "Is that your answer for everything?"

"It's working for me," she said. "You should try it."

"Who do you suggest?" he asked, his voice as cold but conversational—a trap, obviously. "You have someone in mind?"

"There's always Kingsley."

"Kingsley is finally moving on himself," Søren said. "I have never seen him as happy as he is with Juliette."

"Then you've never seen him with you." She crossed her arms tighter across her chest. "Okay, not Kingsley. Someone else. Anyone else. Stop living in the past. I'm not there anymore."

"Eleanor, I'm not going to take another lover simply to assuage your guilt for leaving me."

"No, you're going to play the heartbroken celibate martyr until I come back to you out of guilt. Now you've fucked me and you've fucked Kingsley since becoming a priest so don't pretend to be a saint or a virgin or worse—monogamous. The only reason you haven't moved on and found someone else to love is because you know if you do, then I'll finally be able to move on, too. This is one more example of your sadism."

"That's an astute observation, Little One. You're more intelligent than you look."

"Do I look stupid today for some reason?"

"You're standing outside in forty-degree weather with no shoes on. You've certainly looked more intelligent than you do now."

Nora's fingers curled into a fist. One of these days he was going to be on the receiving end of her sadism, and he wasn't going to like it.

"Have you ever considered the possibility I want you to find someone else to love for you? For your sake?" she asked, trying to stay calm.

"No."

Nora laughed although she found none of this funny.

"Anyone on earth..." she began and stopped. She had to take a deep breath before she could start again. "Anyone on earth would be blessed to be loved by you. I was. Maybe I want you to move on and find someone else for her sake."

"Or you could stop running from me."

"This isn't running," she said looking down at her bare feet that ached on the cold floor of her porch. "This is standing. Standing and living my life. I'm not your property anymore."

"You still love me."

"So? I love this, too. I'm not ready to give this up yet. I'm just finding out who I am finally."

"Mine," Søren said. "You are mine. That's who you are."

"And you wonder why I'm not running back to you?"

He looked her up and down and smiled coldly to himself. "Put your shoes on, Eleanor."

And without another word, he turned and walked away.

She didn't give him the satisfaction of watching him go. She stepped back into her house, shut and locked the door behind her and winced in agony.

He was right. She should have put on some fucking shoes. Standing outside barefoot in forty-degree weather was incredibly stupid.

Nora stood with her back to her front door stamping her feet and waiting for the pins in her feet sensation to fade.

She raised her hand to her face and wiped away an unwelcome tear with her fingertips. She hated fighting with Søren. Play-fighting was one thing. Saying "I hate you, you big blond asshole" was one thing. Acting like they were archenemies for the amusement of The 8th Circle's denizens was one thing.

This was another thing entirely. And it hurt.

She looked at the two beer bottles on her coffee table. The first time she'd gone to Europe she'd been with Søren. The trip was a gift from Kingsley to them both. Søren was a wine drinker, not a beer drinker. Except, he'd said to her, the Trappist monks in Belgium made the most perfect beer in the world. If Christ had turned water into beer instead of wine it would taste like Achel Blonde. He'd taken her to Denmark to meet his family, Belgium to drink their beer, Germany to visit her ancestral stomping grounds, and Paris because Kingsley had grown up there and she'd wanted to see his old house, his old neighborhood, his old life he'd left behind. Those were the two most perfect weeks of her life. And then they'd come back to America, back to Connecticut, back to Søren being a Catholic priest, back to her being his dirty little secret.

She never forgot that trip, never stopped drinking that perfect Belgian beer, never forgot how hard it was to come home. In Europe when he was off-duty, they'd walked in the sunlight together. Back in America, she could see him only at night, only in secret, only in the shadows.

Pain no longer needled her feet. She picked up the bottles off the coffee table, poured the contents down her kitchen drain , and threw the empties into the recycling bin. She'd yelled at Søren for living in the past.

Maybe she should take her own advice. Right now.

She walked back to her bedroom and found Lance still sleeping. He looked pretty damn comfortable in her bed. Too comfortable. She woke him up with a few bites on his shoulders, a few bites on his chest.

His eyelashes fluttered open and Nora raised a finger to her lips, bidding him to remain quiet. As she bit him and nibbled on him, he managed to stay silent but for a few tight intakes of air.

She bit a path up to his ear and kissed it before whispering, "Two nights ago you made me come using just your mouth and no hands. Now you get to use your hands...but nothing else. Understand?"

Lance didn't take the bait. He didn't reply in words; he merely nodded a yes. Nora slipped out of her robe and straddled his naked hips. Pleased with his ability to follow orders, she gave him a kiss on the mouth before rolling onto her back. Lance took two pillows and put one under her head and the other under her hips. Her legs fell wide open and she relaxed into the warmth of the setting sunlight streaming through the windows and the comfort of being with a man who she trusted, a man who wanted nothing but to give her pleasure again and again. More women should really try the domme lifestyle. A man genetically programmed to want to sexually service a woman and be her willing slave? She had yet to find the downside.

Settling between her open thighs, Lance stroked her legs, massaged her stomach and hips.

"Toys are in the drawer," Nora said. "And lube. Anything you want. You don't have to use them, but in case you were wondering..."

Lance raised his eyebrow and tentatively opened the drawer of her nightstand. He looked in the drawer and his eyes widened hugely before looking back at her. He stuck his hand in the drawer, winced, and blew on his fingers as if something had burned him. Nora covered her face and laughed again. She couldn't remember the last time she'd laughed so hard in bed with a man. Usually, it was get in, get kinky, get laid and get out. Or with Søren it was get in, cry, get beaten, cry, get laid, try not to cry when she remembered how much she missed him, and get out.

With his hand playing the part of a creeping spider, Lance slowly and carefully dipped his hand once more into the drawer.

"Lube and a vibrator?" she asked. "You take this orgasm stuff seriously, don't you?"

Lance nodded. He held three fingers up.

"Is that what you're putting in me?" she asked, pointing at his hand.

He shook his head no.

"Is that how many times you're going to get me off?"

This time he nodded.

"Groovy," she said and fluffed her pillow behind her head. "Go for it."

He went for it. First, he did nothing but touch her with his bare hands. He slid two fingers into her and she sighed as he pushed deep, probing her. He widened her with his fingertips, and found the most secret places inside her, even going far enough in to lightly touch her cervix.

He pulled his fingers out but only long enough to pour some lubricant on them before going back in. Now instead of two fingers, he pushed in three. Three and then four. And with his thumb, he teased her clitoris.

Heat pooled in her stomach and she knew Lance could feel it radiating between her thighs. She loved the touch of a man's hand inside her, opening her up in different ways, turning her inside out with pleasure. Lance moved his hand with a spiraling motion, spiraling in and out again, in and out. She wanted to beg for release, but she remembered that she was the dominant partner here and had to act like it. So instead of begging, she ordered.

"Lance, if you don't stop teasing me, I will get out the butt plugs and the hot sauce."

That threat did the trick. Lance pressed against her swollen clitoris and rubbed it. Nora raised her hips and came hard around his hand.

She held up one finger.

"One down, two to go," she said. Lance gave her a smile so male, so arrogant she almost had multiple orgasms.

He held up two fingers in a peace sign. He didn't seem the least intimidated by the prospect of giving her two more. She did like her men dexterous and confident. A fantastic combination.

While she recovered from her first orgasm, Lance massaged her stomach before turning his attentions to her breasts. He rolled her nipples between his fingers and thumbs until the peaks had turned ruddy and hard. She closed her eyes as he toyed with her breasts. Every time he pinched her nipples, new ecstasy spiked into her stomach and made her hyperaware of her clitoris. When she started to pant again, Lance stopped and turned on the vibrator.

Nora kept her eyes closed as he slid the vibrator into her. He'd chosen the largest, thickest one in the drawer and her body opened, stretching to take it all in. The low buzz of it sent delicious waves of heat deep into her. Lance needed to do nothing except gently tease her clitoris to bring her to a second, even more powerful orgasm.

After her second climax of their game peaked and waned, Nora almost called off number three.

"If you make me come again it might kill off the last of whatever brain cells I have left," she warned Lance. Those two orgasms had been face-meltingly good.

Lance gave a nonchalant shrug as if he couldn't care less that her I.Q. dropped precipitously for every intense climax he gave her. According to the tests she had I.Q. points to spare. Why not?

"Well, you used your fingers and you used a vibrator. What tricks do you have up your sleeve for number three?" she asked.

Using both hands Lance motioned her to flip over. She gave him a suspicious look before complying.

Lance lifted her hips so she had to come up onto her knees. Then with both hands, he parted her thighs. Resting on her elbows Nora felt him moving to sit right before her.

"Just hands," she reminded him. "No mouth or cock."

He spread her thighs even wider. Nora arched her back and waited. Once more she heard the flipping of the lid on the lubricant but this time Lance poured out a copious amount into his palm.

She had a mirror on the back of her closet door. With her head turned she could watch what he did to her. Nothing better than starring in and watching porn at the same time.

Lance smoothed the lubricant onto her inner lips but that wasn't the only part of her that got his attention. He pressed two fingers of one hand into her anally and then three fingers of his other hand into her vagina. Working in tandem, both hands massaged inside her as she panted and moaned into the sheets. She felt split open and violated and loved every second of it.

Lance pressed down and pushed up inside her and Nora flinched from the pleasure. Working his fingers in wide spirals, he scraped her inner walls with just enough pressure to send her to the edge of ecstasy again. A fourth finger pushing into her sent her right over. She dug her hands into the sheets and came hard and loud.

Carefully Lance pulled out of her as she crumbled onto the bed, spent and laughing.

"Oh, my God..." she breathed, rolling onto her back. "I think you killed me. Am I dead? You can talk again."

"You're not dead."

"That's a relief. I have stuff to do."

"I don't want to go to prison for killing you with orgasms. I'd really never get to see my kid again."

Nora laughed, low and tired. "All you would have to do is give the women of the jury orgasms like that and you'd get a life sentence chained to their bed."

"I'd rather spend my life chained to your bed."

Lance crawled over Nora's spent body and

kissed her long and deep. He pulled back and she looked up at him.

"I gotta get some damn chains."

They napped again and when Nora woke up she found the bed empty. She didn't worry. Lance could be in the bathroom, in the kitchen. She hadn't given him permission to leave so she knew she would find him somewhere in the house.

She dragged herself from her bed and picked her gray robe off the floor.

A pleasant sort of soreness suffused her hips and lower back. Sex with both Søren and Lance in less than twenty-four hours? She knew some people might disapprove but she couldn't care less. In fact, she decided she deserved a medal for her distinguished sexual service to mankind. At least a Purple Something to match her purple bruises.

Quietly and on bare feet, she padded down the stairs following the sound of Lance's voice. He seemed to be on the phone somewhere so she didn't want to interrupt. She'd much rather eavesdrop.

She found him in her kitchen sitting at the table wearing nothing but his jeans again. He had his cell phone to his ear and his back to the door.

"How's school going?" he asked. "Do you like your teacher?"

He paused and Nora smiled, knowing his daughter was on the other end of the line.

"That's good. She sounds nice. Whose birthday was it?"

Again a pause.

"That sounds like so much fun," he agreed, his voice going so soft and tender Nora's heart tightened as if someone had wrapped a fist around it. "I'm jealous. I want to play in a bouncy house, too."

Lance listened again for a moment.

"No, Daddy can't come to your school party. I know, baby. I know. Daddy's so sorry he can't make it...No, don't be mad at Mommy, this isn't her fault. She wants you to be happy, too."

Nora covered her mouth with her hand to silence her tears. She saw Lance's back heaving as he raised a hand to his face. She couldn't stand seeing men cry—not unless it was in her dungeon. Her own father hadn't given two shits about her. Oh, he'd put on a good act, an act she'd believe for sixteen years until he finally showed his true colors. But she knew in her heart he'd never cared enough about her to shed a single tear over her. He hadn't even tried for joint custody when her parents divorced. That should have been her first sign that her dad hadn't wanted her. If he'd once sat at a kitchen table on the phone in the dark weeping because he couldn't see her, she would have forgiven him everything.

"I'll send you a present," Lance promised his daughter. "Anything you want. As long as it's not a pony. Or a puppy."

He laughed softly at whatever she answered.

"Okay, not a kitten, either," he said. "Do you

want anything that isn't alive and walks around on four legs? Maybe I'll just surprise you."

Lance fell silent again as Lance's daughter apparently took control of the conversation, likely listing everything she wanted for her birthday.

"Be a good girl for Daddy," he whispered. "I'll see you as soon as I can, I promise...I love you, too, my Maya."

Lance ended the call and put the phone on the table in front of him. Nora took a deep breath, one deep enough he heard it and spun around.

"Get dressed," Nora ordered. "We're going to the city."

"What are we doing?" he asked, standing up and coming to her.

"We're doing what I'm always doing— breaking the rules."

She was the dominant in this relationship so she didn't have to explain anything. She gave the orders. Lance followed them. Life was simpler in a D/s relationship.

Nora halted in the middle of shoving her feet into her shoes. Had she really just used the word "relationship"?

Yes. Yes, she had. But only in her mind, she comforted herself. Didn't count until she said it out loud. And a "relationship" wasn't that scary, was it? She had a working relationship with her hairstylist. She had an adversarial relationship with her dentist. *Relationship* wasn't a dirty word. Nothing to be afraid of. Not like it was *monogamy*.

Still, she kept her guard up as she and Lance drove into New York. She refused to tell him where they were going, knowing Lance would probably try to talk her out of it.

"Are you going to at least tell me what rule we're breaking this evening?" Lance asked as they made their way through Manhattan traffic.

"Kingsley has a rule," she said as she turned onto the street she'd been seeking. "More of a guideline. No...it's definitely a rule. He runs the show, he's the king. We, his lovely employees, are his ambassadors to his kingdom. And often we're his bait. My clients are very wealthy, very powerful, very influential, and important. Kingsley says that these people honor us with a sacred trust. We provide them a valuable service that the rest of the world doesn't quite understand and in return they pay us exorbitant sums of money. And sometimes they pay us with more than money."

"Like what?"

"Information, assistance...the usual. But Kingsley wants to handle that sort of stuff. We ambassadors just put on a good face for the empire. But I'm cutting Kingsley out. I need to ask a favor of a client."

"Two questions—what client? And will you get in trouble for this?"

"Two answers—Judge Bollinger," she said as they pulled into the side street near his house and parked. "And yes, big trouble."

PART V: THE LAST GOOD NIGHT

Nora marched right up to the judge's front door and rang the bell.

"Nora, I don't want you getting into trouble for me." Lance took her hand. "Let's go. I can figure my own problems out."

"You can go if you want, but I'm staying. I'm not happy unless I'm getting in trouble. Don't you want me to be happy?" She gave him her most ingratiating, innocent, and utterly fake smile.

"You're evil."

"Well...obviously." She patted him on the cheek as patronizingly as she could. Mrs. B. opened the door and gave Nora a look of surprise.

"Hello there, dear. I didn't think you had an appointment tonight." Mrs. B. ushered Nora and Lance inside.

"No appointment. Is the judge home? I need to talk to him about a legal issue."

"Did you get arrested again?" Mrs. B looked like a worried mother hen.

"No, I promise. Not this week. Not yet, anyway."

"That's good to hear," Mrs. B said. "The judge is in his office. Go on in."

Nora thanked the woman, and she and Lance headed back down the hall. Nora found Judge B at his desk, his nose buried in a massive legal tome. He gave her a beatific smile as she walked in.

"Miss Nora, what brings you here?" He came around his desk, and kissed Nora on the cheek.

"I need a favor, Judge. Or maybe just legal advice."

"Did you get arrested again?" he asked, giving her a stern look.

"Why does everyone always ask me that? Don't answer that," she said. "Judge B., this is Lance. He's my bodyguard, and he's got a problem. Tell him your problem, sailor."

"I'm all ears," Judge B said, motioning Nora and Lance to sit. They moved books off the chairs and sat down while the judge sat on the edge of the desk and gave them his full attention.

Lance told the judge the same story he'd told Nora—the quick marriage, the deployment, the daughter, the wound in his back and the surgeries, the wife who'd withheld sex, the pornography and the custody fight, the only fight Lance had ever lost.

The judge nodded as he listened, asked a few

questions here and there. At the end they all sat in silence waiting for the judge's verdict.

"Son..." the judge finally said, "you got screwed."

Lance laughed and shook his head. "I did and it was the worst sex I ever had."

"All this over some porn?" Judge B. sounded disgusted. "Who doesn't watch porn?"

"Blind people?" Nora offered her best and only guess. "And Lance wasn't even watching the really good porn."

"Subspace.com?" the judge asked, sound disappointed. Personal experience, no doubt.

"That. Can't stand that tame shit," Nora said. "The good stuff's on Kinkster.com."

"It's pay-per-view, though." Judge B. said.

"But it's worth every penny. They've got the best group sex vid on there. Lots of feet action."

"Can you send me the link?"

"Excuse me," Lance interjected. "Are we talking about my legal situation or where to find the best kinky porn?"

"Why can't we talk about both?" Nora asked Lance who replied with only a glare. "Fine, back on subject. So Lance got screwed. What can he do about it?"

The judge adjusted his glasses as he spoke.

"I can help. Definitely. If everything you've told me is true—"

"It is," Lance said.

"Then there is some hope. I know the judge

you had—Hawkins? Hate that self-righteous bastard. He sides with the mothers in ninety-five percent of his cases no matter what the circumstances. I can suggest a good attorney, and we'll get your case moved to another judge. We'll have to petition the court for a new hearing based on new circumstances—"

"What new circumstances?" Lance asked. "Nothing's really changed."

"Considering your fitness as a parent was called into question, you'll probably need a psychiatric evaluation, a thorough one. Once the psych eval clears you of being an unfit parent, then you'll have plenty of ammunition in your fight."

"I can do that, definitely. You think it'll work?"

The judge nodded. "Yes. Once we get you in a new courtroom, which I can handle, and your attorney presents your psych eval and any other new evidence...should at least get you joint custody."

"That's all I want. I don't want to take Maya from her mom."

"That attitude is the right one to have. This battle is *for* your daughter, not *against* your ex-wife. A bad attitude can doom a case. But speaking of dooming a case..."

Judge B. turned his gaze from Lance and onto Nora.

"What?" Nora asked. "What did I do this time?"

"You exist," Judge B. said.

"That's not my fault," Nora said. "I didn't ask

to be born. Which is good because my mother probably would have said no."

The judge gave a tired, nervous laugh.

"My dear...I could not be more grateful that you exist," he said. "But am I correct in assuming this young man is slightly more than just a bodyguard?"

"We did have sex today. A lot of it," she admitted without shame.

"That's going to be an issue." The judge looked from Nora to Lance. Nora felt her stomach starting to tighten with fear.

"How much of an issue?" Lance reached out and took Nora's hand. The touch comforted her, but her stomach remained taut with worry.

"A big one. This beautiful young lady lives and works on the outskirts of legality. She assaults people for money and is paid in cash, probably under the table."

"I take the Fifth." Nora's stomach knot twisted tighter.

"Does he know the rest?" the judge asked her and Nora winced.

"No. Not yet."

"There's a rest?" Lance looked at her with a gaze that said "You've gotta be kidding me." "You mean more than you being a professional dominatrix?"

"Sort of," she said.

"More than sort of." The judge walked over to his bookcase and ran his hands along the spines. He pulled out a rather battered-looked paperback novel. Nora held her breath. "Here you go, son. Ever read the books by this lovely lady?"

Lance stared at the cover. "*The Runaway* by... Nora Sutherlin. Nora, you write books?"

"I am exercising my right to remain silent."

"Guilty on all charges. And I might throw the book at you." Judge B. tossed her book at her. "Even if no one in the courtroom knew about Miss Nora's moonlighting as a dominatrix, it's public record that she's an erotica writer."

"I had no idea you were famous," Lance said, looking both impressed and concerned.

"I'm a writer. I'm the opposite of famous."

"Infamous," the judge supplied. "Shall I tell him what the book's about or will you?"

"I write my own copy all the time. I'll do it. It's loosely based on the story of Daphne and Apollo, except in this case Daphne is a sixteen-year-old girl who lives in a group home and is being pursued by the handsome older off-duty cop who accidentally killed her violent twin brother while restraining him during a fight. It's actually a sweet love story. You know, apart from all the statutory rape."

Lance buried his face in his hands.

"In a child custody case, everything is evidence including the works of fiction written by the father's new girlfriend."

"You're not helping my case here, Judge B."

Nora pointed her finger at him. He raised his hands in surrender.

"You wanted the truth and my help. I'm simply telling it like it is." The judge sighed heavily. "Of course, it does get worse."

"Worse?" Lance's eyes widened in horror. "What's worse?"

"The lovely Miss Nora works for Kingsley Edge who I assume you also work for, yes?"

"Yes," Lance said, his lips tightening into a thin line of worry.

"Kingsley Edge is the last person in this city you want to be involved with when fighting for custody of a child. No matter his virtues as an individual, his enterprise is slightly...What's the word I'm looking for?"

"*Illegal,*" Nora said, swallowing a hard knot in the throat.

"More than that," the judge continued, "it's dangerous. With that much money involved, that many important people who have a lot to lose are involved...let's just say it's not going to reflect well on you to be on his payroll."

"So I quit the job?" Lance asked. Nora could hear the disappointment in his words, the reluctance.

"You'll have to if you want your daughter back. You're no longer in the Navy?"

"No. Medical discharge. Honorable discharge," he said.

"Were you awarded any medals?"

"Maybe," he said and left it at that.

"That's good. I can make sure we get you a new judge, a judge who has a military background. As a veteran, a wounded and decorated veteran, you should have a very good chance for equal custody. Have you considered rejoining the Navy?"

"Not really an option. I was offered a job in defense contracting from a company that works with the Navy in Rhode Island."

"With SPECWAR?" Nora asked.

Lance narrowed his eyes at her. "How do you know about that?"

Nora mimed locking her lips and throwing away the key.

"Don't ask, don't tell." She had a rather important client there she would hate to piss off. Damn good tipper.

"How's the pay?" the judge asked Lance.

"Stellar. But it's a desk job. I like to be active. That's why I wanted to work for Kingsley running security at his clubs, helping people in a hands-on way. Sitting in front of a computer isn't my idea of serving people."

"It might be worth swallowing your pride over. Getting your paycheck from a legitimate employer will reflect much better on you than a paycheck from Kingsley Edge. There's no bones about it, young man. I can get you in front of a sympathetic judge, I can help you find a good lawyer, I can tell you which psychologist to call for your psych eval, but the rest is up to you. If you want your daughter back, you're going to have to say goodbye to this world, goodbye to your job with Kingsley and goodbye to Mistress Nora."

Lance fell silent. Nora looked up at Judge B. who could only smile apologetically at her. She leaned forward and squeezed his hand, grateful for his honesty even if his honesty hurt.

"So let me get this straight..." Lance stood up and started to pace the small cluttered office. "I have dreamed for two years about getting my daughter back. I have dreamed for sixteen years about finding the perfect woman for me. I find the perfect woman for me and find out how to get my daughter back, but...to get my daughter back, I have to give up the perfect woman."

"If it makes you feel any better," Nora said, turning to face him, "I'm not the perfect woman." If Lance thought she was perfect, maybe they should go their separate ways.

"Perfect or not," Judge B. said, "you are correct. Being involved with her would give your ex-wife's attorney all the ammunition they need to keep you away from your daughter. Is it fair? No, not at all. I have nine grandchildren and would let Miss Nora babysit for them in a heartbeat. But what is fair is rarely a question the courts bother answering. What is right is often thrown under the bus in favor of what *looks* right."

"But you're a client of hers." Lance faced the

judge and pointed at Nora. "How is it okay for you to be involved with her and not me?"

"That's a good question but with an ugly answer. I'm a judge, you aren't. Also, I have money and influence, and I'm only a year or two away from retirement. I could retire tomorrow, but I love my work and feel like I still have something to offer. My children are grown and they all have an inkling about my interests so they'd hardly be shocked by a scandal. They certainly would never try to keep my grandchildren from me. If it came to light that I saw this lovely lady once a week, I'd retire early, taking some ribbing from friends and colleagues, and move down to Boca with my wife."

Lance sat back down again with a heavy sigh.

"There's no other way?" he asked, looking up at the judge with imploring eyes.

"Son, I wish I could tell you something different. I wish I could tell you that there weren't two sets of rules out there for rich, important people like me and normal people like you. I wish I could tell you there wasn't a separate set of rules for men and women. I could tell you that but it would be a lie and you know it. And lying to you won't help you get your daughter back."

"What do I do now?" Lance asked after a long and heavy silence.

"You get out of this world and you don't look back," Judge B. said. "Cut off contact with her, with Kingsley Edge, with the entire community. You get your psych evaluation to prove you're a fit

parent. Take the job with a civilian defense con-
tractor if it pays well and looks good for the
courts."

"But Lance is kinky," Nora protested, ready to
scream at the unfairness. "That's like telling a gay
man to be straight so he can have custody of his
kid."

"Yes, and if that gay man wanted custody of
his child badly enough he'd do it or at least put on
a damn good show for the court. Look, I'm not
saying you have to give up this lifestyle forever. If
in a year or two after you win custody back you
find a nice girl who has a job at a bank or is a
schoolteacher...and she just happens to enjoy role-
play in the bedroom, then that's fine. It's between
you two. You won't do it while your daughter's in
the house. You won't leave any evidence of it lying
around. But you running around town with a professional dominatrix who writes hard-core erotica
and gets arrested every other week is going to get
you and your case laughed right out of court."

"I have to do it now?" Lance asked, and Nora's
heart broke at the question. Broke for him and
broke for her. She already knew the answer before
the judge gave it to them.

"I would suggest it. The sooner the better. The
more time you spend with her the more likely it is
someone will find out, the more likely your ex-wife
will find out. There's no privacy in this world anymore. The Internet has killed that fantasy. All it
takes is one person knowing or one picture or one

rumor spreading...your ex-wife can hire a private detective and get all the evidence she needs in an hour to keep you away from your daughter. Most judges don't know their asses from a hole in the ground, so trying to explain the difference between a dominatrix and a prostitute...Well, you'd have a better chance teaching me how to tap-dance on the moon. Or teaching Miss Nora here..."

"Math," she suggested. "I'm really bad at math."

"Here's some math even you can do then," the judge said, giving her a kind but hopeless smile. "You plus Lance equals no custody for his daughter."

Nora swallowed a hard lump in her throat. "I fucking hate math."

Nora and Lance thanked the judge for his honesty and his time, and they left the house with nothing but heavy hearts and another bag of Mrs. B.'s chocolate chip cookies.

"What do you want to do?" Nora asked once inside the car. "I can take you home."

"I don't want to go home." Lance leaned his head against the window. "I want to go to your house, spend the night with you, and never leave your bed again."

"I want that, too." Nora put her hand on his knee and squeezed. "But you heard what Judge B. said."

"I heard."

"Lance...Listen to me. This is your Mistress talking."

"Fine, I'm listening."

"I'm crazy about you. But we just met a few days ago. The sex is amazing and you're amazing, but this is something bigger than both of us."

"I know. I know I'll do it."

"Of course you will. But not yet." She took the exit.

"Are you kidnapping me?" Lance asked as they left the city.

"Don't tempt me. I just might. I'll knock you out and when you wake up we'll be in the middle of nowhere France in a beautiful little cottage with all the bondage and S&M equipment we could ever need."

"Sounds like heaven."

"It is heaven. Except it's a *No Children Allowed* sort of Heaven. Is that your version of heaven?"

"No."

"Thought so."

Once they entered Wakefield, Nora had to consciously force herself to drive in the opposite direction of Sacred Heart, Søren's church...her church. Instead, she steered her car a mile away into a small residential neighborhood on the outskirts of town.

"Where are we?" Lance asked as she parked in a cul-de-sac in front of a shabby pre-fab duplex with sickly pale green aluminum siding and a dead lawn. Behind the cul-de-sac stood a wall of trees, windblown and tired.

"It doesn't look any better now than when I lived here." Nora got out of the car and leaned back against the door.

"You used to live here?"

"Yup. Grew up in this house." She pointed at the left side of the duplex.

"It's..." Lance paused and Nora laughed.

"Shitville, USA?"

"I didn't say that," Lance raised his hand.

"You didn't have to. Admittedly, it's not like I grew up in the projects or anything. Just on the wrong side of the tracks. Anyway, it's not pretty. It's worse on the inside."

"Worse?"

"It's probably the one bad neighborhood in this entire town. But no one lives here anymore. Not in the house or the neighborhood."

She looked up and down the street and saw only a car or two parked and no signs of life.

"Why not?" he asked.

Nora started to answer but closed her mouth when the sound of an oncoming train started up in the distance. She smiled at Lance and put her hands in her jacket pockets.

"One..." she said, counting the seconds, "two... three...Brace yourself."

At the end of the three, the train barreled past with ear-splitting loudness. Lance covered his ears but Nora only waited it out.

"What the fuck?" Lance lowered his hands from his ears.

"The railroad tracks are right behind the trees here. I grew up with that sound—every day and every night. I can still sleep through a hail storm because I grew up with that in my backyard."

"You've got to be kidding me."

Nora shook her head.

"Nope. A decade ago a train derailed about fifty yards that way." She pointed east. "It was carrying some nasty chemicals on it. This entire neighborhood was evacuated. Lots of people moved out then and never moved back."

"Is it safe to be here?"

"It's clean now. But no one wants to live near the tracks."

"I can't blame them." Lance kicked a rock in the front lawn.

"Me neither. It was nothing but plastic plates and plastic cups growing up. We literally could not have nice things in our house. They'd fall off the table and break into a thousand pieces. When I bought my house, the one you've been in, the first thing I did was buy a whole set of crystal glasses and vases and everything I could get my hands on, the more breakable the better. I like having things I can break, knowing they'll only break when I want them to."

"Not because you live right on the train tracks."

"Exactly."

"Were you happy here?" Lance stepped onto the sidewalk and Nora followed. So weird to be back in this neighborhood. So many memories came rushing over her that she felt she could drown in their murky depths.

"I did okay here," she said. "I never learned how to ride a bike. I got one, a pink Schwinn, but it got stolen before I could learn to ride it. We couldn't afford a new one. I cared more about motorcycles than bicycles by that point, anyway."

"You lived here with your parents?"

"My mom." Nora walked up to the front door. She peered in a window and saw the emptiness inside—no furniture, no people, no life.

"Where was your dad?"

"The Iron Triangle in Queens. That's where his chop shop was. Or he was in jail. I was a baby when my mom realized her mechanic husband actually ran a chop shop. She left him. They got divorced and Mom refused any child support. She didn't want my father anywhere near me."

"I don't blame her. God, I can't imagine growing up like this." He pointed at the decrepit house, the abandoned neighborhood. "I can't imagine growing up with my father in prison. Dad... he and I are buddies. He was a sub commander, not that you'd ever know it. A very humble man."

"Sub commander? Sounds like me. Different sort of subs, obviously."

"Submarines," Lance said, laughing. "He was

on his last deployment right before the Gulf War broke out. Instead of coming home, he stayed in. I think that's the one time I remember my mom breaking down while Dad was away. She was already planning his welcome home party."

"God damn, that must have been hard." Nora took his hand in hers.

"It was. I asked him about it, asked him if he was angry he had to stay in. He said he wasn't. He knew Mom had things under control, that my sister and I were doing fine. He said..."

Lance paused and swallowed. A smile flitted across his face.

"My dad said that there comes a time when what you want to do is the opposite of what you need to do. And the boys do what they want to do, but the men..." Lance stood up a little straighter. "The men do what they need to do."

"I see where you get all your annoying nobility from."

"No, Dad's one of a kind. He says I'm his hero. I say the same about him."

"You're lucky to have a great father, such great parents. Mom and I butted heads from day one. I was my father's daughter. When I was thirteen, fourteen, I'd run off to Queens any chance I could to see him. I'd take a bus, take the subway, surprise him at his shop. He'd treat me like his little princess, take me to lunch with his friends, then drive me home. He wasn't a real parent, never disciplined me or anything. Mom did all the work so I hated her and loved him."

"What happened? I mean, to him and you."

Nora turned away from the window, the empty house, the memories.

"I got in trouble. Big, bad trouble. My father ran for the hills and left me hanging, even though it was his fault I was in all that trouble. Søren stepped in and took care of me as best as he could. But I wasn't my father's little girl anymore. And then Dad was dead, and I didn't miss him."

Lance stood in silence and stared at the house.

"I have no regrets about how my life turned out," Nora said, coming to stand next to him. "But if I could wave a magic wand and grow up with a father as loving and caring and protective as you, I'd wave the hell out of it."

"You would?"

"In a heartbeat. There are two types of teenage rebellion—the normal kind and the kind that gets you in juvenile detention. Mine was of the latter variety. And I know if I'd had a normal father, a good father, that wouldn't have been the case."

"I want to be a good father to my daughter. You know I do." Lance squeezed her hand before letting it go again.

"When a girl feels abandoned by her dad, she might latch onto an older man who takes an interest in her. Luckily for me, this other man I latched on to took great care of me. He got me out of trouble and kept me out of trouble. It could have just as easily been a sleaze I fell for who knocked me up and left me stranded again. I know a few girls who went down that path."

Lance rubbed his chin, that half a day's stubble she found so enticing. But she kept her hands to herself, knowing the next time she touched him would be the last time she touched him.

"I could get my daughter back," Lance finally said.

"You could. Judge B. sounded pretty optimistic. He knows everyone in family court, has lots of pull. He'll be able to help you."

"I'm grateful to him. It's just..." Lance turned and looked at her and in his dark blue eyes, she saw the road they'd never take, not together anyway. And it would have been a lovely stroll down that road. The entire Underground would have turned out for the party when their infamous Mistress Nora finally settled down and put a collar on a sub. The women would swoon over handsome, noble, chivalrous Lance and the men would admire him for being man enough to take her on. She could see the mornings ahead of them: the breakfasts Lance would serve to her in bed, the tea he'd bring to her office while she worked on a book, the neck rubs he'd give her when she spent too much time sitting at her desk or too long flogging a client. She could imagine how devastatingly debonair

Lance would look in a tuxedo when they attended a formal party at Kingsley's or a special event her publisher hosted. And the nights...all those nights in bed with Lance serving her every sexual whim and Nora treating him to his every desire... They could live a lifetime of good nights together. He could give her everything she wanted. She could give him everything he needed. And no one could take that away from them.

"I have to do what I need to do," Lance said at last. "Even if it's not what I want to do."

"One last good night?" Nora offered. It was all she had to give.

Lance nodded instead of speaking. They drove in silence to her house and in silence they entered it. In silence they kissed and in silence she led him to the bedroom.

All night long he lavished attention on her body. He spent an hour kissing and teasing her breasts. She spent another hour beating him black and blue with her floggers, single-tails, and canes. For his sake, she wanted to leave him with bruises that would last for weeks. For her sake, she wanted to know that he would carry the imprint of their time together on his body. She tied him down and rode him until she'd exhausted herself and him with orgasms. Then they slept...but only for a while.

Nora awoke in the hour before dawn. She stared at Lance's sleeping form. Of all the men she'd let in this bed none looked more right in it than Lance. A mix of moonlight and streetlight snuck into the room and revealed the welts and bruises that decorated Lance's broad, muscled back.

Willpower alone kept her from kissing one beautiful and blackening bruise under his shoulder blade. Instead of touching him or kissing him, she pulled away and tiptoed to her closet. She slipped into a sheer black negligee she'd bought months ago but hadn't worn yet. Why not? No better time than now. Now was all they had. But she wasn't finished digging yet. Somewhere in this mess of a walk-in closet...she knew it was here...yes. She found it. The black velvet bag she'd hidden away.

From the top of her closet, she pulled down a candle box and a lighter. As Lance slept she lit six of the candles and set them about the room. She had no plans for wax-play unless he asked her for it. She merely wanted to see his body by candle-light for the first and last time.

At last she had the room ready. Sunrise was still an hour away.

Standing at the side of the bed Nora paused, picked up a candle, and bent forward. Her lips touched Lance's shoulder the second the hot wax landed on his back.

Lance twitched and came awake in an instant and sat up. Panting from the shock of the painful awakening, he stared at Nora and said nothing, waiting like a well-trained soldier for the next command.

Nora only stared at him for a moment, at the veins in his forearms, the lines of lean muscle in his stomach and chest, the scattering of scars that only added to his allure. She set the candle back on the table. She picked up the black velvet bag, opened the silver drawstring and pulled out a heavy leather collar.

Lance looked down at the collar and then back at her with a question in his eyes. Nora turned it in her hand, tilting it toward the light.

"There's this Israeli leatherworker that Kingsley knows. He makes all of Kingsley's whips and floggers. Old guy. Probably knew Moses. Anyway..." Nora traced the ornate silver buckle on the back of the collar. "He had this with him last time he was at Kingsley's. I bought it. One of those love-at-first-sight, impulse buys." She smiled at Lance who seemed to be barely breathing now. Nora's words, although whispered, seemed to echo off the walls. "The craftsmanship is incredible. See the grooves on it? It's engraved. He said it's the Hebrew words for *protector. Provider. Slave.* He's a romantic old soul. I didn't have anyone in mind when I bought it. I just wanted it."

"Why?" Lance asked, still staring at the collar but not touching it.

"I don't know. Why do girls who don't have boyfriends buy bridal magazines? They buy them to dream, I guess. Even dominatrixes have dreams."

"I wish I could make your dreams come true, Mistress."

"You can. For an hour maybe. Dreams don't last long. They don't even last the whole night."

"How? I'll do anything."

"Wear this for me. Accept it. Be mine until morning since that's all we have left."

"It's not enough time."

"How much would be enough?" she asked, not expecting an answer. "The longer we put this off, the more it will hurt, the more people who will know about us. You know she's more important to you than I am. You know she has to be."

Lance nodded reluctantly.

Nora unbuckled the lock on the collar. "Until dawn?" she asked. "Just until then?"

"Yes. Better an hour in paradise than a lifetime outside the walls."

"Come inside," she said and raised the collar.

"Are you sure? You shouldn't waste something—"

She laid her hand on the side of his face and caressed his stubble with her thumb.

"The night we met you gave the bartender a ten-dollar tip for seven dollars' worth of beer at a club where the alcohol is free and the only guys who tip the server are trying to get her in bed which you weren't. Yes, I'm sure. And no, it's not a waste."

Lance raised no more objections. He leaned forward and rested his forehead head on her shoulder. Nora locked the collar around his neck and he sat up straight again. As she knew it would, it fit Lance perfectly. Never in her twelve years in the Underground had she seen a more handsome collared sub. The collar drew attention to the muscles in his shoulders and his powerful neck. He looked stronger in it, not weaker, more manly, not less.

"You're mine." She kissed his lips. "My property. My possession. My slave and servant. My knight and my protector."

"Yours," he said and seemingly could say no more.

Nora placed her hands on either side of his neck, feeling his pulse beating against the leather collar.

"Make love to me any way you want. Whatever your fantasy is, whatever your dream, live it with me now. Don't worry if I'll like it or not, because I'm with you. I know I'll love it."

Lance slid out of the bed and stood behind her. He pressed his naked body against her back. Nora's hips were flush with the bed. Against her lower back she felt his erection, impossibly hard and thick. He kissed the side of her neck and the leather of the collar scraped her skin, a sensation so surprising and erotic that chills passed through her all the way to her feet. For one brief moment, she thought of Søren. Had he relished the feel of her collar on his shoulder or chest as she lay under him? Did he miss it now that she no longer wore it?

Lance's hands on her breasts sent thoughts of all other men scattering. He cupped them through the thin fabric of her negligee and her nipples hardened, puckering against his fingers.

"Standing?" she asked as he slid the straps of her gown down her arms, baring her breasts. "From behind? That's the fantasy?" She wasn't disappointed or displeased, merely curious why he'd chosen this way for their last time together.

He kissed her earlobe as he pinched her nipples, waves of pleasure shooting into her stomach.

"Standing so I can protect you." He ran a hand through her long hair and shoved a fistful of it off the back of her neck. "From behind so I can shield you."

She understood at once what he meant. If someone broke into the house while they were making love, Lance's body would stand between her and the intruder at the door. Even during sex he would keep her safe or die trying.

Lance kissed the back of her neck, kissed his way down her spine. Kneeling, he caressed the back of her thighs with his mouth. He lifted her gown and kissed her bottom, back, and hips. Slipping a hand between her legs, he spread her folds with his fingertips, teased the taut knot of her clitoris, and she dampened against his hand.

He stood again and pressed his whole body

into hers. She parted her thighs wider as he angled himself against her inner lips. He didn't enter her at first, simply sliding along the length of her opening as she bathed him in her wetness and need.

She clutched at the sheets as he lifted his hips and thrust up and into her. Their bodies merged seamlessly as he sank deeper and deeper into her wet warmth. Lance's hot breath scalded her skin as he pushed into her with endless patience and controlled force. One strong hand held her naked hip. The heel of his other hand pushed into her belly creating delicious pressure in her entire pelvic region. The pressure rose in waves, clutching at her insides as she moved with and into Lance's thrusts.

She felt her body tightening around him. Nora bent over the bed, pushed back, and took him deeper into her. She wanted all of him she could take, all of him she could get.

Lance thrust faster into her, moving with short sharp jabs that she felt in the pit of her stomach as he grasped her swollen clitoris between his thumb and forefinger and massaged it. It should be like this every night...But this would be the last night.

Now she desired nothing more than release. She tensed as Lance wrapped his arm around her chest and held her so close only their hips moved together. With a hoarse cry and a shudder that wracked her whole body, Nora came hard, her vaginal muscles latching onto Lance still moving inside her.

Spent now, she placed her hands on the bed to hold herself steady as Lance pushed into her. He held her by her hips as he moved with long hard strokes that took him almost completely out of her before plunging back into her again. One more thrust and he climaxed, his hands gripping Nora's hips with viselike force. She hoped he'd leave bruises on her, bruises on her body to match the one on her heart.

He stayed embedded in her long enough for both of them to catch their breath. Finally, he eased out of her and Nora turned to face him. It was done now. It was over. The sun was rising. Their last night together had ended.

She ordered him to shower and he did. She ordered him to get dressed and he did. When she told him to keep the collar, he accepted it with such humble gratitude she had to cover his mouth with her hand to stop him from speaking. If he said one more beautiful thing to her she'd never let him go.

When she ordered him to leave her and not look back...

"I don't know if I can follow that order," he said, standing at her door, his hand on the knob.

"You can. You will."

"I'll try to find another way," Lance pledged. "If there's any way I can come back and still have my daughter, I'll find it."

"I know you will," she said and knew she would never see him again. There was no other way. And even if there was, by the time he found it she would have moved on and so would he. But they cared about each other too much right now to admit the truth that they both knew. "Go get your little lady back. She needs your protection more than I do."

"Yes, Mistress." Lance stood a moment on the porch, and it took everything Nora had to keep from crying. "Mistress?"

"What, sailor?"

"This may sound stupid, but this felt like something. You and me, I mean. Something planned. I'm not the only one who felt like this was destiny, right?"

Nora raised her chin and smiled.

"A wise man once told me that destiny doesn't always play matchmaker," she said. "Sometimes it plays other games with us. Sometimes we win the game..."

"Sometimes we lose."

"You know...I'm not the only one of my kind. There are other dommes out there. Some of us don't even charge for our services."

"Other Mistress Noras? I don't believe it."

"I'm the only Mistress Nora I know and the world says 'thank God' to that, but...I'm just saying you only have to play their stupid game until you get your kid back. Then you can date again. You can find another one of us. You're too good of a sub to waste yourself on some boring vanilla who doesn't know what she has. Any domme would be honored to have you on her arm, at her feet. You'll find someone amazing. I know you will."

"Maybe. Who knows? Destiny might play matchmaker someday. Maybe destiny will get it right next time."

"I wish..." Nora began and stopped. She knew what she wanted to say. She wanted to say *I wish it could be me*. But those words would hurt as much to say as they would to hear. She left them safely unsaid, knowing that Lance wasn't her destiny. She'd already met her destiny and three years ago she'd told her destiny goodbye. She survived it. She would survive this, too.

Lance said nothing more. Nora knew he waited for another kiss, a kiss she couldn't trust herself to give. So he smiled at her one more time before walking to his car, getting in, and driving off. He left as ordered, and as ordered, he didn't look back.

"Good boy," she whispered before correcting herself. "Good man."

Nora watched him go before she shut the door, locked it, and returned to her bed. It took an hour before she could sleep again, and just as she feared, when she woke up, Lance was gone from her life forever. Such was the nature of dreams. They only feel endless in the dream. By dawn they turn to dust.

For a week, Nora went through the motions of life —sleeping, eating, working, and then starting over again the next day. She had her weekly appointment with Judge B., but they didn't talk about Lance. She spent the night at Kingsley's, and he mentioned he'd found a new head of security for his clubs. She visited Natasha at her apartment and found the pretty purpled-haired dominatrix itching to get back to work. The client who had robbed and assaulted her would be charged with everything the DA could throw at him. Nora suggested Natasha come back to work for Kingsley for the sake of safety in numbers. Natasha admitted it wasn't a bad idea and promised she would think about it.

The Wednesday of that week Nora drove back to Wakefield and attended daily Mass. She didn't stay to talk to Søren, she didn't talk to anyone. She sat in the back, stayed kneeling during Communion, and only smiled at him once as she walked out the door of her old church and back again into her new life.

That night Nora found herself back at The 8th Circle bar.

"Okay, Kool-Aid. I got this. Try me." Nora sipped at her drink and took a deep breath.

"Are you sure about this, Mistress?" Simone laid her hand on Nora's thigh and gave it a reassuring squeeze. "I mean really sure about it?"

"I'm so unbelievably sure right now that I'm stuck to the stool. Just ask me. I've got this."

"If you insist. Here we go... How old are you, Mistress Nora?"

"I am thirty years old."

"And...how much do you weigh?"

Nora took another deep breath. She opened her mouth and then closed it again. "Maybe I don't got this."

"Mistress..." Simone laughed and laid her rainbow-hued head onto Nora's shoulder. "It's okay. I don't like telling people how much I weigh, either."

"I don't care how much you weigh. I just want to know what the hell kind of chemicals you're using on your hair. Is that shit even legal? Are you giving yourself a brain tumor?"

"I don't think so," Simone sat up and rubbed her head. "I don't feel any brain tumors. Although I have recently forgotten the last half of the alphabet and my own phone number. Is that a sign of a tumor?"

"Sounds more like Jäger than a tumor. I think you'll live."

"Thank God. I have a date tonight."

"With whom? That big blond guy again?"

Simone shook her head. "With the most beautiful dominatrix in the entire Underground. I hope she'll have me."

Nora gave the girl the side-eye. "Most beautiful dominatrix in the Underground? Fuck that bitch, you're spending the night with me."

Simone laughed as Nora put her finger in Simone's house collar and dragged her off the barstool.

"Come on, Kool-Aid," Nora said. "Let's go play a game of hide the dildo."

"I love that game. No matter who wins, I always win," Simone said.

Nora led her toward the elevator at the edge of the bar. They'd play a little in the pit tonight to get the girl warmed up before Nora dragged her back to the dungeon and did wonderful terrible things to her all night long.

The elevator rose and Søren stepped out and into the bar.

"Excuse us, sir," Nora said. "We'll be needing that elevator."

"Where are you going with Simone?" He stared down at Nora who only smiled up at him.

"Where am I going? Third base, for starters."

"She and I did not get to finish our evening together. We were interrupted." Søren looked down at Nora coldly with a dark gleam in his eyes. She had to fight off a smile. So he'd forgiven her for their little fight on the porch then? Good. They couldn't play-fight like this when they were actually mad at each other.

"Sorry. Not my fault." Nora started to brush past him.

"Eleanor..."

"Mistress Nora, we did get interrupted," Simone said rather sheepishly.

"Thank you, dear," Søren said and held out his hand to Simone. Simone looked imploringly at Nora.

"You know the rules, Blondie. Call Kingsley," Nora said to Søren. Simone leaned into Nora and gave her a kiss on the cheek. "Make an appointment."

The two women boarded the elevator and headed down.

"Thank you, Mistress. I've been dying to play with you for weeks. You're so brave. He looked grumpy."

"Søren doesn't scare me."

"You're my knight in shining armor, Mistress." Simone gave a playfully melodramatic sigh and laid her head on Nora's shoulder.

"I knew a knight once," Nora said as the elevator hit the floor and they stepped out into the darkness. "I've got nothing on him."

THE END.

ACKNOWLEDGMENTS

This story was inspired by true events. Unfortunately kinky people losing custody of their children is not, in fact, a work of pure fiction.

Thank you to Angie of the Smut Book Club, Taylor Lunsford, and Karen Stivali for their editing expertise. Very special thanks to Elizabeth Belchik for all her naval fact-checking. Thank you to the U.S. Navy. God bless you all.

ABOUT THE AUTHOR

Tiffany Reisz is the *USA Today* bestselling author of the Romance Writers of America RITA®-winning Original Sinners series.

Her erotic fantasy *The Red* —the first entry in the Godwicks series, self-published under the banner 8th Circle Press—was named an NPR Best Book of the Year and a Goodreads Best Romance of the Month.

Tiffany lives in Kentucky with her husband, author Andrew Shaffer, and their cat. The cat is not a writer.

Subscribe to the Tiffany Reisz email newsletter to stay up-to-date with new releases, ebook discounts, and signed books:

www.tiffanyreisz.com/mailing-list

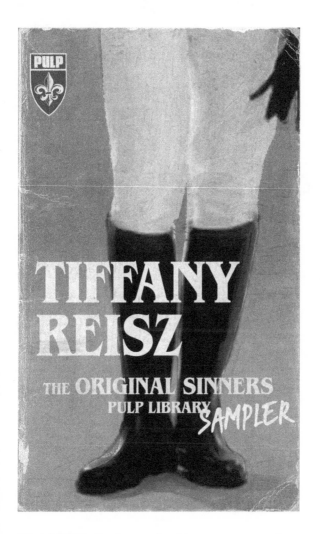

This **FREE** ebook sampler features excerpts from
seven Original Sinners Pulp Library titles. Download at www.tiffanyreisz.com or wherever ebooks
are sold.

SACRED HEART CATHOLIC CHURCH

SINNERS WELCOME